Back to God's Country

AND OTHER STORIES

James Oliver Curwood

1st WORLD
LIBRARY
Literary Society

Back to God's Country
and other stories

James Oliver Curwood

© 1st World Library – Literary Society, 2004
PO Box 2211
Fairfield, IA 52556
www.1stworldlibrary.org
First Edition

LCCN: 2004091222

Softcover ISBN: 1-59540-660-3
eBook ISBN: 1-59540-760-X

Purchase *"Back To God's Country"*
as a traditional bound book at:
www.1stWorldLibrary.org/purchase.asp?ISBN=1-59540-660-3

1st World Library Literary Society is a nonprofit
organization dedicated to promoting literacy by:

- Creating a free internet library accessible from any computer worldwide.
- Hosting writing competitions and offering book publishing scholarships.

Readers interested in supporting literacy
through sponsorship, donations or
membership please contact:
literacy@1stworldlibrary.org
Check us out at: www.1stworldlibrary.org

Back to God's Country

contributed by the Charles Family
in support of
1st World Library Literary Society

CONTENTS

BACK TO GOD'S COUNTRY

When Shan Tung, the long-cued Chinaman from Vancouver, started up the Frazer River in the old days when the Telegraph Trail and the headwaters of the Peace were the Meccas of half the gold-hunting population of British Columbia, he did not foresee tragedy ahead of him. He was a clever man, was Shan Tung, a cha-sukeed, a very devil in the collecting of gold, and far-seeing. But he could not look forty years into the future, and when Shan Tung set off into the north, that winter, he was in reality touching fire to the end of a fuse that was to burn through four decades before the explosion came.

With Shan Tung went Tao, a Great Dane. The Chinaman had picked him up somewhere on the coast and had trained him as one trains a horse. Tao was the biggest dog ever seen about the Height of Land, the most powerful, and at times the most terrible. Of two things Shan Tung was enormously proud in his silent and mysterious oriental way - of Tao, the dog, and of his long, shining cue which fell to the crook of his knees when he let it down. It had been the longest cue in Vancouver, and therefore it was the longest cue in British Columbia. The cue and the dog formed the combination which set the forty-year fuse of romance and tragedy burning. Shan Tung started for the El Dorados early in the winter, and Tao alone pulled his sledge and outfit. It was no more than an ordinary task for the monstrous Great Dane, and Shan Tung subserviently but with hidden triumph passed outfit after outfit exhausted by the way. He had reached Copper Creek Camp, which was boiling and frothing with the excitement of gold-maddened men, and was congratulating himself that he would soon be at the camps west of the Peace, when the thing happened. A drunken Irishman, filled with a grim and unfortunate sense of humor, spotted Shan Tung's wonderful cue and coveted it. Wherefore there followed a bit of excitement in which Shan Tung passed into his empyrean home with a bullet through his heart, and the drunken Irishman was strung up for his misdeed fifteen minutes later. Tao, the Great Dane, was taken by the leader of the men who pulled on the rope. Tao's new master was a "drifter," and as he drifted, his face was always set to the north, until at last a new humor struck him and he turned eastward to the Mackenzie. As the seasons passed, Tao found mates along the way and left a string of his progeny behind him, and he had new masters, one after another, until he was grown old and his muzzle was turning gray. And never did one of these masters turn south with him. Always it was north, north with the white man first, north with the Cree, and then wit h the Chippewayan, until in the end the dog born in a Vancouver kennel died in an Eskimo igloo on the Great Bear. But the breed of the Great Dane lived on. Here and there, as the years passed, one would find among the Eskimo trace-dogs, a grizzled-haired, powerful-jawed giant that was alien to the arctic stock, and in these occasional aliens ran the blood of Tao, the Dane.

Forty years, more or less, after Shan Tung lost his life and his cue at Copper Creek Camp, there was born on a firth of Coronation Gulf a dog who was named Wapi, which means "the Walrus." Wapi, at full growth, was a throwback of more than forty dog generations. He was nearly as large as his forefather, Tao. His fangs were an inch in length, his great jaws could crack the thigh-bone of a caribou, and from the beginning the hands of men and the fangs of beasts were against him. Almost from the day of his birth until this winter of his fourth year, life for Wapi had been an unceasing fight for existence. He was maya-tisew - bad with the badness of a devil. His reputation had gone from master to master and from igloo to igloo; women and children were afraid of him, and men always spoke to him with the club or the lash in their hands. He was hated and feared, and yet because he could run down a barren-land caribou and kill it within a mile, and would hold a big white bear at bay until the hunters came, he was not sacrificed to this hate and fear. A hundred whips and clubs and a hundred pairs of hands were against him between Cape Perry and the crown of Franklin Bay - and the fangs of twice as many dogs.

The dogs were responsible. Quick-tempered, clannish with the savage brotherhood of the wolves, treacherous, jealous of leadership, and with the older instincts of the dog dead within them, their merciless feud with what they regarded as an interloper of another breed put the devil heart in Wapi. In all the gray and desolate sweep of his world he had no friend. The heritage of Tao, his forefather, had fallen upon him, and he was an alien in a land of strangers. As the dogs and the men and women and children hated him, so he hated them. He hated the sight and smell of the round-faced, blear-eyed creatures who were his master, yet he obeyed them, sullenly, watchfully, with his lips wrinkled warningly over fangs which had twice torn out the life of white bears. Twenty times he had killed other dogs. He had fought them singly, and in pairs, and in packs. His giant body bore the scars of a hundred wounds. He had been clubbed until a part of his body was deformed and he traveled with a limp. He kept to himself even in the mating season. And all this because Wapi, the Walrus, forty years removed from the Great Dane of Vancouver, was a white man's dog.

Stirring restlessly within him, sometimes coming to him in dreams and sometimes in a great and unfulfilled yearning, Wapi felt vaguely the strange call of his forefathers. It was impossible for him to understand. It was impossible for him to know what it meant. And yet he did know that somewhere there was something for which he was seeking and which he never found. The desire and the questing came to him most compellingly in the long winter filled with its eternal starlight, when the maddening yap, yap, yap of the little white foxes, the barking of the dogs, and the Eskimo chatter oppressed him like the voices of haunting ghosts. In these long months, filled with the horror of the arctic night, the spirit of Tao whispered within him that somewhere there was light and sun, that somewhere there was warmth and flowers, and running streams, and voices he could understand, and things he could love. And then Wapi would whine, and perhaps the whine would bring him the blow of a club, or the lash of a whip, or an Eskimo threat, or the menace of an Eskimo dog's snarl. Of the latter Wapi was unafraid. With a snap of his jaws, he could break the back of any other dog on Franklin Bay.

Such was Wapi, the Walrus, when for two sacks of flour, some tobacco, and a bale of cloth he became the property of Blake, the uta-wawe-yinew, the trader in seals, whalebone - and women. On this day Wapi's soul took its flight back through the space of forty years. For Blake was white, which is to say that at one time or another he had been white. His skin and his appearance did not betray how black he had turned inside and Wapi's brute soul cried out to him, telling him how he had waited and watched for this master he knew would come, how he would fight for him, how he wanted to lie down and put his great head on the white man's feet in token of his fealty. But Wapi's bloodshot eyes and battle-scarred face failed to reveal what was in him, and Blake - following the instructions of those who should know - ruled him from the beginning with a club that was more brutal than the club of the Eskimo.

For three months Wapi had been the property of Blake, and it was now the dead of a long and sunless arctic night. Blake's cabin, built of ship timber and veneered with blocks of ice, was built in the face of a deep pit that sheltered it from wind and storm. To this cabin came the Nanatalmutes from the east, and the Kogmollocks from the west, bartering their furs and whalebone and seal-oil for the things Blake gave in exchange, and adding women to their wares whenever Blake announced a demand. The demand had been excellent this winter. Over in Darnley Bay, thirty miles across the headland, was the whaler Harpoon frozen up for the winter with a crew of thirty men, and straight out from the face of his igloo cabin, less than a mile away, was the Flying Moon with a crew of twenty more. It was Blake's business to wait and watch like a hawk for such opportunities as there, and tonight - his watch pointed to the hour of twelve, midnight - he was sitting in the light of a sputtering seal-oil lamp adding up figures which told him that his winter, only half gone, had already been an enormously profitable one.

"If the Mounted Police over at Herschel only knew," he chuckled. "Uppy, if they did, they'd have an outfit after us in twenty-four hours."

Oopi, his Eskimo right-hand man, had learned to understand English, and he nodded, his moon-face split by a wide and enigmatic grin. In his way, "Uppy" was as clever as Shan Tung had been in his.

And Blake added, "We've sold every fur and every pound of bone and oil, and we've forty Upisk wives to our credit at fifty dollars apiece."

Uppy's grin became larger, and his throat was filled with an exultant rattle. In the matter of the Upisk wives he knew that he stood ace-high.

"Never," said Blake, "has our wife-by-the-month business been so good. If it wasn't for Captain Rydal and his love-affair, we'd take a vacation and go hunting."

He turned, facing the Eskimo, and the yellow flame of the lamp lit up his face. It was the face of a remarkable man. A black beard concealed much of its cruelty and its cunning, a beard as carefully Van-dycked as though Blake sat in a professional chair two thousand miles south, but the beard could not hide the almost inhuman hardness of the eyes. There was a glittering light in them as he looked at the Eskimo. "Did you see her today, Uppy? Of course you did. My Gawd, if a woman could ever tempt me, she could! And Rydal is going to have her. Unless I miss my guess, there's going to be money in it for us - a lot of it. The funny part of it is, Rydal's got to get rid of her husband. And how's he going to do it, Uppy? Eh? Answer me that. How's he going to do it?"

In a hole he had dug for himself in the drifted snow under a huge scarp of ice a hundred yards from the igloo cabin lay Wapi. His bed was red with the stain of blood, and a trail of blood led from the cabin to the place where he had hidden himself. Not many hours ago, when by God's sun it should have been day, he had turned at last on a teasing, snarling, back-biting little kiskanuk of a dog and had killed it. And Blake and Uppy had beaten him until he was almost dead.

It was not of the beating that Wapi was thinking as he lay in his wallow. He was thinking of the fur-clad figure that had come between Blake's club and his body, of the moment when for the first time in his life he had seen the face of a white woman. She had stopped Blake's club. He had heard her voice. She had bent over him, and she would have put her hand on him if his master had not dragged her back with a cry of warning. She had gone into the cabin then, and he had dragged himself away.

Since then a new and thrilling flame had burned in him. For a time his senses had been dazed by his punishment, but now every instinct in him was like a living wire. Slowly he pulled himself from his retreat and sat down on his haunches. His gray muzzle was pointed to the sky. The same stars were there, burning in cold, white points of flame as they had burned week after week in the maddening monotony of the long nights near the pole. They were like a million pitiless eyes, never blinking, always watching, things of life and fire, and yet dead. And at those eyes, the little white foxes yapped so incessantly that the sound of it drove men mad. They were yapping now. They were never still. And with their yapping came the droning, hissing monotone of the aurora, like the song of a vast piece of mechanism in the still farther north. Toward this Wapi turned his bruised and beaten head. Out there, just beyond the ghostly pale of vision, was the ship. Fifty times he had slunk out and around it, cautiously as the foxes themselves. He had caught its smells and its sounds; he had come near enough to hear the voices of men, and those voices were like the voice of Blake, his master. Therefore, he had never gone nearer.

There was a change in him now. His big pads fell noiselessly as he slunk back to the cabin and sniffed for a scent in the snow. He found it. It was the trail of the white woman. His blood tingled again, as it had tingled when her face bent over him and her hand reached out, and in his soul there rose up the ghost of Tao to whip him on. He followed the woman's footprints slowly, stopping now and then to listen, and each moment the spirit in him grew more insistent, and he whined up at the stars. At last he saw the ship, a wraithlike thing in its piled-up bed of ice, and he stopped. This was his dead-line. He had never gone nearer. But tonight - if any one period could be called night - he went on.

It was the hour of sleep, and there was no sound aboard. The foxes, never tiring of their infuriating sport, were yapping at the ship. They barked faster and louder when they caught the scent of Wapi, and as he approached, they drifted farther away. The scent of the woman's trail led up the wide bridge of ice, and Wapi followed this as he would have followed a road, until he found himself all at once on the deck of the Flying Moon. For a space he was startled. His long fangs bared themselves at the shadows cast by the stars. Then he saw ahead of him a narrow ribbon of yellow light. Toward this Wapi sniffed out, step by step, the footprints of the woman. When he stopped again, his muzzle was at the narrow crack through which came the glimmer of light.

It was the door of a deck-house veneered like an igloo with snow and ice to protect it from cold and wind. It was, perhaps, half an inch ajar, and through that aperture Wapi drank the warm, sweet perfume of the woman. With it he caught also the smell of a man. But in him the woman scent submerged all else. Overwhelmed by it, he stood trembling, not daring to move, every inch of him thrilled by a vast and mysterious yearning. He was no longer Wapi, the Walrus; Wapi, the Killer. Tao was there. And it may be that the spirit of Shan Tung was there. For after forty years the change had come, and Wapi, as he stood at the woman's door, was just dog, - a white man's dog - again the dog of the Vancouver kennel - the dog of a white man's world.

He thrust open the door with his nose. He slunk in, so silently that he was not heard. The cabin was lighted. In a bed lay a white-faced, hollow-cheeked man - awake. On a low stool at his side sat a woman. The light of the lamp hanging from above warmed with gold fires the thick and radiant mass of her hair. She was leaning over the sick man. One slim, white hand was stroking his face gently, and she was speaking to him in a voice so sweet and soft that it stirred like wonderful music in Wapi's warped and beaten soul. And then, with a great sigh, he flopped down, an abject slave, on the edge of her dress.

With a startled cry the woman turned. For a moment she stared at the great beast wide-eyed, then there came slowly into her face recognition and understanding. "Why, it's the dog Blake whipped so terribly," she gasped. "Peter, it's - it's Wapi!" For the first time Wapi felt the caress of a woman's hand, soft, gentle, pitying, and out of him there came a wimpering sound that was almost a sob.

"It's the dog - he whipped," she repeated, and, then, if Wapi could have understood, he would have noted the tense pallor of her lovely face and the look of a great fear that was away back in the staring blue depths of her eyes.

From his pillow Peter Keith had seen the look of fear and the paleness of her cheeks, but he was a long way from guessing the truth. Yet he thought he knew. For days - yes, for weeks - there had been that growing fear in her eyes. He had seen her mighty fight to hide it from him. And he thought he understood.

"I know it has been a terrible winter for you, dear," he had said to her many times. "But you mustn't worry so much about me. I'll be on my feet again - soon." He had always emphasized that. "I'll be on my feet again soon!"

Once, in the breaking terror of her heart, she had almost told him the truth. Afterward she had thanked God for giving her the strength to keep it back. It was day - for they spoke in terms of day and night - when Rydal, half drunk, had dragged her into his cabin, and she had fought him until her hair was down about her in tangled confusion - and she had told Peter that it was the wind. After that, instead of evading him, she had played Rydal with her wits, while praying to God for help. It was impossible to tell Peter. He had aged steadily and terribly in the last two weeks. His eyes were sunken into deep pits. His blond hair was turning gray over the temples. His cheeks were hollowed, and there was a different sort of luster in his eyes. He looked fifty instead of thirty-five. Her heart bled in its agony. She loved Peter with a wonderful love.

The truth! If she told him that! She could see Peter rising up out of his bed like a ghost. It would kill him. If he could have seen Rydal - only an hour before - stopping her out on the deck, taking her in his arms, and kissing her until his drunken breath and his beard sickened her! And if he could have heard what Rydal had said! She shuddered. And suddenly she dropped down on her knees beside Wapi and took his great head in her arms, unafraid of him - and glad that he had come.

Then she turned to Peter. "I'm going ashore to see Blake again - now," she said. "Wapi will go with me, and I won't be afraid. I insist that I am right, so please don't object any more, Peter dear."

She bent over and kissed him, and then in spite of his protest, put on her fur coat and hood, and stood for a moment smiling down at him. The fear was gone out of her eyes now. It was impossible for him not to smile at her loveliness. He had always been proud of that. He reached up a thin hand and plucked tenderly at the shining little tendrils of gold that crept out from under her hood.

"I wish you wouldn't, dear," he pleaded.

How pathetically white, and thin, and weak he was! She kissed him again and turned quickly to hide the mist in her eyes. At the door she blew him a kiss from the tip of her big fur mitten, and as she went out she heard him say in the thin, strange voice that was so unlike the old Peter:

"Don't be long, Dolores."

She stood silently for a few moments to make sure that no one would see her. Then she moved swiftly to the ice bridge and out into the star-lighted ghostliness of the night. Wapi followed close behind her, and dropping a hand to her side she called softly to him. In an instant Wapi's muzzle was against her mitten, and his great body quivered with joy at her direct speech to him. She saw the response in his red eyes and stopped to stroke him with both mittened hands, and over and over again she spoke his name. "Wapi - Wapi - Wapi." He whined. She could feel him under her touch as if alive with an electrical force. Her eyes shone. In the white starlight there was a new emotion in her face. She had found a friend, the one friend she and Peter had, and it made her braver.

At no time had she actually been afraid - for herself. It was for Peter. And she was not afraid now. Her cheeks flushed with exertion and her breath came quickly as she neared Blake's cabin. Twice she had made excuses to go ashore - just because she was curious, she had said - and she believed that she had measured up Blake pretty well. It was a case in which her woman's intuition had failed her miserably. She was amazed that such a man had marooned himself voluntarily on the arctic coast. She did not, of course, understand his business - entirely. She thought him simply a trader. And he was unlike any man aboard ship. By his carefully clipped beard, his calm, cold manner of speech, and the unusual correctness with which he used his words she was convinced that at some time or another he had been part of what she mentally thought of as "an entirely different environment."

She was right. There was a time when London and New York would have given much to lay their hands on the man who now called himself Blake.

Dolores, excited by the conviction that Blake would help her when he heard her story, still did not lose her caution. Rydal had given her another twenty-four hours, and that was all. In those twenty-four hours she must fight out their salvation, her own and Peter's. If Blake should fail -

Fifty paces from his cabin she stopped, slipped the big fur mitten from her right hand and unbuttoned her coat so that she could quickly and easily reach an inside pocket in which was Peter's revolver. She smiled just a bit grimly, as her fingers touched the cold steel. It was to be her last resort. And she was thinking in that flash of the days "back home" when she was counted the best revolver shot at the Piping Rock. She could beat Peter, and Peter was good. Her fingers twined a bit fondly about the pearl-handled thing in her pocket. The last resort - and from the first it had given her courage to keep the truth from Peter!

She knocked at the heavy door of the igloo cabin. Blake was still up, and when he opened it, he stared at her in wide-eyed amazement. Wapi hung outside when

Dolores entered, and the door closed. "I know you think it strange for me to come at this hour," she apologized, "but in this terrible gloom I've lost all count of hours. They have no significance for me any more. And I wanted to see you - alone."

She emphasized the word. And as she spoke, she loosened her coat and threw back her hood, so that the glow of the lamp lit up the ruffled mass of gold the hood had covered. She sat down without waiting for an invitation, and Blake sat down opposite her with a narrow table between them. Her face was flushed with cold and wind as she looked at him. Her eyes were blue with the blue of a steady flame, and they met his own squarely. She was not nervous. Nor was she afraid.

"Perhaps you can guess - why I have come?" she asked.

He was appraising her almost startling beauty with the lamp glow flooding down on her. For a moment he hesitated; then he nodded, looking at her steadily. "Yes, I think I know," he said quietly. "It's Captain Rydal. In fact, I'm quite positive. It's an unusual situation, you know. Have I guessed correctly?"

She nodded, drawing in her breath quickly and leaning a little toward him, wondering how much he knew and how he had come by it.

"A very unusual situation," he repeated. "There's nothing in the world that makes beasts out of men - most men - more quickly than an arctic night, Mrs. Keith. And they're all beasts out there - now - all except your husband, and he is contented because he possesses the one white woman aboard ship. It's putting it brutally plain, but it's the truth, isn't it? For the time being they're beasts, every man of the twenty, and you - pardon me! - are very beautiful. Rydal wants you, and the fact that your husband is dying - "

"He is not dying," she interrupted him fiercely. "He shall not die! If he did - "

"Do you love him?" There was no insult in Blake's quiet voice. He asked the question as if much depended on the answer, as if he must assure himself of that fact.

"Love him - my Peter? Yes!"

She leaned forward eagerly, gripping her hands in front of him on the table. She spoke swiftly, as if she must convince him before he asked her another question. Blake's eyes did not change. They had not changed for an instant. They were hard, and cold, and searching, unwarmed by her beauty, by the luster of her shining hair, by the touch of her breath as it came to him over the table.

"I have gone everywhere with him - everywhere," she began. "Peter writes books, you know, and we have gone into all sorts of places. We love it - both of us - this adventuring. We have been all through the country down there," she swept a hand to the south, "on dog sledges, in canoes, with snowshoes, and pack-trains. Then we hit on the idea of coming north on a whaler. You know, of course, Captain Rydal planned to return this autumn. The crew was rough, but we expected that. We expected to put up with a lot. But even before the ice shut us in, before this terrible night came, Rydal insulted me. I didn't dare tell Peter. I thought I could handle Rydal, that I could keep him in his place, and I knew that if I told Peter, he would kill the beast. And then the ice - and this night - " She choked.

Blake's eyes, gimleting to her soul, were shot with a sudden fire as he, too, leaned a little over the table. But his voice was unemotional as rock. It merely stated a fact. "That's why Captain Rydal allowed himself to be frozen in," he said. "He had plenty of time to get into the open channels, Mrs. Keith. But he wanted you. And to get you he knew he would have to lay over. And if he laid over, he knew that he would get you, for many things may happen in an arctic night. It shows the depth of the man's feelings, doesn't it? He is sacrificing a great deal to possess you, losing a great deal of time, and money, and all that. And when your husband dies - "

Her clenched little fist struck the table. "He won't die, I tell you! Why do you say that?"

"Because - Rydal says he is going to die."

"Rydal - lies. Peter had a fall, and it hurt his spine so that his legs are paralyzed. But I know what it is. If he could get away from that ship and could have a doctor, he would be well again in two or three months."

"But Rydal says he is going to die."

There was no mistaking the significance of Blake's words this time. Her eyes filled with sudden horror. Then they flashed with the blue fire again. "So - he has told you? Well, he told me the same thing today. He didn't intend to, of course. But he was half mad, and he had been drinking. He has given me twenty-four hours."

"In which to - surrender?"

There was no need to reply.

For the first time Blake smiled. There was something in that smile that made her flesh creep. "Twenty-four hours is a short time," he said, "and in this matter, Mrs. Keith, I think that you will find Captain Rydal a man of his word. No need to ask you why you don't appeal to the crew! Useless! But you have hope that I can help you? Is that it?"

Her heart throbbed. "That is why I have come to you, Mr. Blake. You told me today that Fort Confidence is only a hundred and fifty miles away and that a Northwest Mounted Police garrison is there this winter - with a doctor. Will you help me?"

"A hundred and fifty miles, in this country, at this time of the year, is a long distance, Mrs. Keith," reflected Blake, looking into her eyes with a steadiness that at any other time would have been embarrassing. "It means the McFarlane, the Lacs Delesse, and the Arctic Barren. For a hundred miles there isn't a stick of timber. If a storm came - no man or dog could live. It is different from the coast. Here there is shelter everywhere." He spoke slowly, and he was thinking swiftly. "It would take five days at thirty miles a day. And the chances are that your husband would not stand it. One hundred and twenty hours at fifty degrees below zero, and no fire until the fourth day. He would die."

"It would be better - for if we stay - " she stopped, unclenching her hands slowly.

"What?" he asked.

"I shall kill Captain Rydal," she declared. "It is the only thing I can do. Will you force me to do that, or will you help me? You have sledges and many dogs, and we will pay. And I have judged you to be - a man."

He rose from the table, and for a moment his face was turned from her. "You probably do not understand my position, Mrs. Keith," he said, pacing slowly back and forth and chuckling inwardly at the shock he was about to give her. "You see, my livelihood depends on such men as Captain Rydal. I have already done a big business with him in bone, oil, pelts - and Eskimo women."

Without looking at her he heard the horrified intake of her breath. It gave him a pleasing sort of thrill, and he turned, smiling, to look into her dead-white face. Her eyes had changed. There was no longer hope or entreaty in them. They were simply pools of blue flame. And she, too, rose to her feet.

"Then - I can expect - no help - from you."

"I didn't say that, Mrs. Keith. It shocks you to know that I am responsible. But up here, you must understand the code of ethics is a great deal different from yours. We figure that what I have done for Rydal and his crew keeps sane men from going mad during the long months of darkness. But that doesn't mean I'm not going to help you - and Peter. I think I shall. But you must give me a little time in which to consider the matter - say an hour or so. I understand that whatever is to be done must be done quickly. If I make up my mind to take you to Fort Confidence, we shall start within two or three hours. I shall bring you word aboard ship. So you might return and prepare yourself and Peter for a probable emergency."

She went out dumbly into the night, Blake seeing her to the door and closing it after her. He was courteous in his icy way but did not offer to escort her back to the ship. She was glad. Her heart was choking her with hope and fear. She had measured him differently this time. And she was afraid. She had caught a glimpse that had taken her beyond the man, to the monster. It made her shudder. And yet what did it matter, if Blake helped them?

She had forgotten Wapi. Now she found him again close at her side, and she dropped a hand to his big head as she hurried back through the pallid gloom. She spoke to him, crying out with sobbing breath what she had not dared to reveal to Blake. For Wapi the long night had ceased to be a hell of ghastly emptiness, and to her voice and the touch of her hand he responded with a whine that was the whine of a white man's dog. They had traveled two-thirds of the distance to the ship when he stopped in his tracks and sniffed the wind that was coming from shore. A second time he did this, and a third, and the third time Dolores turned with him and faced the direction from which they had come. A low growl rose in Wapi's throat, a snarl of menace with a note of warning in it.

"What is it, Wapi?" whispered Dolores. She heard his long fangs click, and under her hand she felt his body grow tense. "What is it?" she repeated.

A thrill, a suspicion, shot into her heart as they went on. A fourth time Wapi faced the shore and growled before they reached the ship. Like shadows they went up over the ice bridge. Dolores did not enter the cabin but drew Wapi behind it so they could not be seen. Ten minutes, fifteen, and suddenly she caught her breath and fell down on her knees beside Wapi, putting her arms about his gaunt shoulders. "Be quiet," she whispered. "Be quiet."

Up out of the night came a dark and grotesque shadow. It paused below the bridge, then it came on silently and passed almost without sound toward the captain's quarters. It was Blake. Dolores' heart was choking her. Her arms clutched Wapi, whispering for him to be quiet, to be quiet. Blake disappeared, and she rose to her feet. She had come of fighting stock. Peter was proud of that. "You slim wonderful little thing!" he had said to her more than once. "You've a heart in that pretty body of yours like the general's!" The general was her father, and a fighter. She thought of Peter's words now, and the fighting blood leaped through her veins. It was for Peter more than herself that she was going to fight now.

She made Wapi understand that he must remain where he was. Then she followed after Blake, followed until her ears were close to the door behind which she could already hear Blake and Rydal talking.

Ten minutes later she returned to Wapi. Under her hood her face was as white as the whitest star in the sky. She stood for many minutes close to the dog, gathering her courage, marshaling her strength, preparing herself to face Peter. He must not suspect until the last moment. She thanked God that Wapi had caught the taint of Blake in the air, and she was conscious of offering a prayer that God might help her and Peter.

Peter gave a cry of pleasure when the door opened and Dolores entered. He saw Wapi crowding in, and laughed. "Pals already! I guess I needn't have been afraid for you. What a giant of a dog!"

The instant she appeared, Dolores forced upon herself an appearance of joyous excitement. She flung off her coat and ran to Peter, hugging his head against her as she told him swiftly what they were going to do. Fort Confidence was only one hundred and fifty miles away, and a garrison of police and a doctor were there. Five days on a sledge! That was all. And she had persuaded Blake, the trader, to help them. They would start now, as soon as she got him ready and Blake came. She must hurry. And she was wildly and gloriously happy, she told him. In a little while they would be at least on the outer edge of this horrible night, and he would be in a doctor's hands.

She was holding Peter's head so that he could not see her face, and by the time she jumped up and he did see it, there was nothing in it to betray the truth or the fact that she was acting a lie. First she began to dress Peter for the trail. Every instant gave her more courage. This helpless, sunken-cheeked man with the hair graying over his temples was Peter, her Peter, the Peter who had watched over her, and sheltered her, and fought for her ever since she had known him, and now had come her chance to fight for him. The thought filled her with a wonderful exultation. It flushed her cheeks, and put a glory into her eyes, and made her voice tremble. How wonderful it was to love a man as she loved Peter! It was impossible for her to see the contrast they made - Peter with his scrubby beard, his sunken cheeks, his emaciation, and she with her radiant, golden beauty. She was ablaze with the desire to fight. And how proud of her Peter would be when it was all over!

She finished dressing him and began putting things in their big dunnage sack. Her lips tightened as she made this preparation. Finally she came to a box of revolver cartridges and emptied them into one of the pockets of her under-jacket. Wapi flattened out near the door, watched every movement she made.

When the dunnage sack was filled, she returned to Peter. "Won't it be a joke on Captain Rydal!" she exulted. "You see, we aren't gong to let him know anything about it." She appeared not to observe Peter's surprise. "You know how I hate him, Peter dear," she went on. "He is a beast. But Mr. Blake has done a great deal of trading with him, and he doesn't want Captain Rydal to know the part he is taking in getting us away. Not that Rydal would miss us, you know! I don't think he cares very much whether you live or die, Peter, and that's why I hate him. But we must humor Mr. Blake. He doesn't want him to know."

"Odd," mused Peter. "It's sort of - sneaking away."

His eyes had in them a searching question which Dolores tried not to see and which she was glad he did not put into words. If she could only fool him another hour - just one more hour.

It was less than that - half an hour after she had finished the dunnage sack - when they heard footsteps crunching outside and then a knock at the door. Wapi answered with a snarl, and when Dolores opened the door and Blake entered, his eyes fell first of all on the dog.

"Attached himself, eh?" he greeted, turning his quiet, unemotional smile on Peter. "First white woman he has ever seen, and I guess the case is hopeless. Mrs. Keith may have him."

He turned to her. "Are you ready?"

She nodded and pointed to the dunnage sack. Then she put on her fur coat and hood and helped Peter sit up on the edge of the bed while Blake opened the door again and made a low signal. Instantly Uppy and another Eskimo came in. Blake led with the sack, and the two Eskimos carried Peter. Dolores followed last, with the fingers of one little hand gripped about the revolver in her pocket. Wapi hugged so close to her that she could feel his body.

On the ice was a sledge without dogs. Peter was bundled on this, and the Eskimos pulled him. Blake was still in the lead. Twenty minutes after leaving the ship they pulled up beside his cabin.

There were two teams ready for the trail, one of six dogs, and another of five, each watched over by an Eskimo. The visor of Dolores' hood kept Blake from seeing how sharply she took in the situation. Under it her eyes were ablaze. Her bare hand gripped her revolver, and if Peter could have heard the beating of her heart, he would have gasped. But she was cool, for all that. Swiftly and accurately she appraised Blake's preparations. She observed that in the six-dog team, in spite of its numerical superiority, the animals were more powerful than those in the five-dog team. The Eskimos placed Peter on the six-dog sledge, and Dolores helped to wrap him up warmly in the bearskins. Their dunnage sack was tied on at Peter's feet. Not until then did she seem to notice the five-dog sledge. She smiled at Blake. "We must be sure that in our excitement we haven't forgotten something," she said, going over what was on the sledge. "This is a tent, and here are plenty of warm bearskins - and - and - " She looked up at Blake, who was watching her silently. "If there is no timber for so long, Mr. Blake, shouldn't we have a big bundle of kindling? And surely we should have meat for the dogs!"

Blake stared at her and then turned sharply on Uppy with a rattle of Eskimo. Uppy and one of the companions made their exit instantly and in great haste.

"The fools!" he apologized. "One has to watch them like children, Mrs. Keith. Pardon me while I help them."

She waited until he followed Uppy into the cabin. Then, with the remaining Eskimo staring at her in wonderment, she carried an extra bearskin, the small tent, and a narwhal grub-sack to Peter's sledge. It was another five minutes before Blake and the two Eskimos reappeared with a bag of fish and a big bundle of ship-timber kindlings. Dolores stood with a mittened hand on Peter's shoulder, and bending down, she whispered:

"Peter, if you love me, don't mind what I'm going to say now. Don't move, for everything is going to be all right, and if you should try to get up or roll off the sledge, it would be so much harder for me. I haven't even told you why we're going to Port Confidence. Now you'll know!"

She straightened up to face Blake. She had chosen her position, and Blake was standing clear and unshadowed in the starlight half a dozen paces from her. She had thrust her hood back a little, inspired by her feminine instinct to let him see her contempt for him.

"You beast!"

The words hissed hot and furious from her lips, and in that same instant Blake found himself staring straight into the unquivering muzzle of her revolver.

"You beast!" she repeated. "I ought to kill you. I ought to shoot you down where you stand, for you are a cur and a coward. I know what you have planned. I followed you when you went to Rydal's cabin a little while ago, and I heard everything that passed between you. Listen, Peter, and I'll tell you what these brutes were going to do with us. You were to go with the six-dog team and I with the five, and out on the barrens we were to become separated, you to go on and be killed when you we're a proper distance away, and I to be brought back - to Rydal. Do you understand, Peter dear? Isn't it splendid that we should have forced on us like this such wonderful material for a story!"

She was gloriously unafraid now. A paean of triumph rang in her voice, triumph, contempt, and utter fearlessness. Her mittened hand pressed on Peter's shoulder, and before the weapon in her other hand Blake stood as if turned into stone.

"You don't know," she said, speaking to him directly, "how near I am to killing you. I think I shall shoot unless you have the meat and kindlings put on Peter's sledge immediately and give Uppy instructions - in English - to drive us to Fort Confidence. Peter and I will both go with the six-dog sledge. Give the instructions quickly, Mr. Blake!"

Blake, recovering from the shock she had given him, flashed back at her his cool and cynical smile. In spite of being caught in an unpleasant lie, he admired this golden-haired, blue-eyed slip of a woman for the colossal bluff she was playing. "Personally, I'm sorry," he said, "but I couldn't help it. Rydal - "

"I am sure, unless you give the instructions quickly, that I shall shoot," she interrupted him. Her voice was so quiet that Peter was amazed. "I'm sorry, Mrs. Keith. But - "

A flash of fire blinded him, and with the flash Blake staggered back with a cry of pain and stood swaying unsteadily in the starlight, clutching with one hand at an arm which hung limp and useless at his side.

"That time, I broke your arm," said Dolores, with scarcely more excitement than if she had made a bull's-eye on the Piping Rock range. "If I fire again, I am quite positive that I shall kill you!"

The Eskimos had not moved. They were like three lifeless, staring gargoyles. For another second or two Blake stood clutching at his arm. Then he said,

"Uppy, put the dog meat and the kindlings on the big sledge - and drive like hell for Fort Confidence!" And then, before she could stop him, he followed up his words swiftly and furiously in Eskimo.

"Stop!"

She almost shrieked the one word of warning, and with it a second shot burned its way through the flesh of Blake's shoulder and he went down. The revolver turned on Uppy, and instantly he was electrified into life. Thirty seconds later, at the head of the team, he was leading the way out into the chaotic gloom of the night. Hovering over Peter, riding with her hand on the gee-bar of the sledge, Dolores looked back to see Blake staggering to his feet. He shouted after them, and what he said was in Uppy's tongue. And this time she could not stop him.

She had forgotten Wapi. But as the night swallowed them up, she still looked back, and through the gloom she saw a shadow coming swiftly. In a few moments Wapi was running at the tail of the sledge. Then she leaned over Peter and encircled his shoulders with her furry arms.

"We're off!" she cried, a breaking note of gladness in her voice. "We're off! And, Peter dear, wasn't it perfectly thrilling!"

A few minutes later she called upon Uppy to stop the team. Then she faced him, close to Peter, with the revolver in her hand.

"Uppy," she demanded, speaking slowly and distinctly, "what was it Blake said to you?"

For a moment Uppy made as if to feign stupidity. The

revolver covered a spot half-way between his narrow-slit eyes.

"I shall shoot - "

Uppy gave a choking gasp. "He said - no take trail For' Con'dence - go wrong - he come soon get you."

"Yes, he said just that." She picked her words even more slowly. "Uppy, listen to me. If you let them come up with us - unless you get us to Fort Confidence - I will kill you. Do you understand?"

She poked her revolver a foot nearer, and Uppy nodded emphatically. She smiled. It was almost funny to see Uppy's understanding liven up at the point of the gun, and she felt a thrill that tingled to her finger-tips. The little devils of adventure were wide-awake in her, and, smiling at Uppy, she told him to hold up the end of his driving whip. He obeyed. The revolver flashed, and a muffled yell came from him as he felt the shock of the bullet as it struck fairly against the butt of his whip. In the same instant there came a snarling deep-throated growl from Wapi. From the sledge Peter gave a cry of warning. Uppy shrank back, and Dolores cried out sharply and put herself swiftly between Wapi and the Eskimo. The huge dog, ready to spring, slunk back to the end of the sledge at the command of her voice. She patted his big head before she got on the sledge behind Peter.

There was no indecision in the manner of Uppy'S going now. He struck out swift and straight for the pale constellation of stars that hung over Fort Confidence. It was splendid traveling. The surface of the arctic plain was frozen solid. What little wind there was came from behind them, and the dogs were big and fresh. Uppy ran briskly, snapping the lash of his whip and la-looing to the dogs in the manner of the Eskimo driver. Dolores did not wait for Peter's demand for a further explanation of their running away and her remarkable words to Blake. She told him. She omitted, for the sake of Peter's peace of mind, the physical insults she had suffered at Captain Rydal's hands. She did not tell him that Rydal had forced her into his arms a few hours before and kissed her. What she did reveal made Peter's arms and shoulders grow tense and he groaned in his helplessness.

"If you'd only told me!" he protested. Dolores laughed triumphantly, with her arm about his shoulder. "I knew my dear old Peter too well for that," she exulted. "If I had told you, what a pretty mess we'd be in now, Peter! You would have insisted on calling Captain Rydal into our cabin and shooting him from the bed - and then where would we have been? Don't you think I'm handling it pretty well, Peter dear?"

Peter's reply was smothered against her hooded cheek.

He began to question her more directly now, and with his ability to grasp at the significance of things he pointed out quickly the tremendous hazard of their position. There were many more dogs and other sledges at Blake's place, and it was utterly inconceivable that Blake and Captain Rydal would permit them to reach Fort Confidence without making every effort in their power to stop them. Once they succeeded in placing certain facts in the hands of the Mounted Police, both Rydal and Blake would be done for. He impressed this uncomfortable truth on Dolores and suggested that if she could have smuggled a rifle along in the dunnage sack it would have helped matters considerably. For Rydal and Blake would not hesitate at shooting. For them it must be either capture or kill - death for him, anyway, for he was the one factor not wanted in the equation. He summed up their chances and their danger calmly and pointedly, as he always looked at troubling things. And Dolores felt her heart sinking within her. After all, she had not handled the situation any too well. She almost wished she had killed Rydal herself and called it self-defense. At least she had been criminally negligent in not smuggling along a rifle.

"But we'll beat them out," she argued hopefully. "We've got a splendid team, Peter, and I'll take off my coat and run behind the sledge as much as I can. Uppy won't dare play a trick on us now, for he knows that if I should miss him, Wapi would tear the life out of him at a word from me. We'll win out, Peter dear. See if we don't!"

Peter hugged his thoughts to himself. He did not tell her that Blake and Rydal would pursue with a ten- or twelve-dog team, and that there was almost no chance at all of a straight get-away. Instead, he pulled her head down and kissed her.

To Wapi there had come at last a response to the great yearning that was in him. Instinct, summer and winter, had drawn him south, had turned him always in that direction, filled with the uneasiness of the mysterious something that was calling to him through the years of forty generations of his kind. And now he was going south. He sensed the fact that this journey would not end at the edge of the Arctic plain and that he was not to hunt caribou or bear. His mental formulae necessitated no process of reasoning. They were simple and to the point His world had suddenly divided itself into two parts; one contained the woman, and the other his old masters and slavery. And the woman stood against these masters. They were her enemies as well as his own. Experience had taught him the power and the significance of firearms, just as it had made him understand the uses for which spears, and harpoons, and whips were made. He had seen the woman shoot Blake, and he had seen her ready to shoot at Uppy. Therefore he understood that they were enemies and that all associated with them were enemies. At a word from her he was ready to spring ahead and tear the life out of the Eskimo driver and even out of the dogs that were pulling the sledge. It did not take him long to comprehend that the man on the sledge was a part of the woman.

He hung well back, twenty or thirty paces behind the sledge, and unless Peter or the woman called to him, or the sledge stopped for some reason, he seldom came nearer.

It took only a word from Dolores to bring him to her side.

Hour after hour the journey continued. The plain was level as a floor, and at intervals Dolores would run in the trail that the load might be lightened and the dogs might make better time. It was then that Peter watched Uppy with the revolver, and it was also in these intervals - running close beside the woman - that the blood in Wapi's veins was fired with a riotous joy.

For three hours there was almost no slackening in Uppy's speed. The fourth and fifth were slower. In the sixth and seventh the pace began to tell. And the plain was no longer hard and level, swept like a floor by the polar winds. Rolling undulations grew into ridges of snow and ice; in places the dogs dragged the sledge over thin crusts that broke under the runners; fields of drift snow, fine as shot, lay in their way; and in the eighth hour Uppy stopped the lagging dogs and held up his two hands in the mute signal of the Eskimo that they could go no farther without a rest.

Wapi dropped on his belly and watched. His eyes followed Uppy suspiciously as he strung up the tent on its whalebone supports to keep the bite of the wind from the sledge on which Dolores sat at Peter's feet. Then Uppy built a fire of kindlings, and scraped up a pot of ice for tea-water. After that, while the water was heating, he gave each of the trace dogs a frozen fish. Dolores herself picked out one of the largest and tossed it to Wapi. Then she sat down again and began to talk to Peter, bundled up in his furs. After a time they ate, and drank hot tea, and after he had devoured a chunk of raw meat the size of his two fists, Uppy rolled himself in his sleeping bag near the dogs. A little at a time Wapi dragged himself nearer until his head lay on Dolores' coat. After that there was a long silence broken only by the low voices of the woman and the man, and the heavy breathing of the tired dogs. Wapi himself dozed off, but never for long. Then Dolores nodded, and her head drooped until it found a pillow on Peter's shoulder. Gently Peter drew a bearskin about her, and for a long time sat wide-awake, guarding Uppy and baring his ears at intervals to listen. A dozen times he saw Wapi's bloodshot eyes looking at him, and twice he put out a hand to the dog's head and spoke to him in a whisper.

Even Peter's eyes were filmed by a growing drowsiness when Wapi drew silently away and slunk suspiciously into the night. There was no yapping foxes here, forty miles from the coast. An almost appalling silence hung under the white stars, a silence broken only by the low and distant moaning the wind always makes on the barrens. Wapi listened to it, and he sniffed with his gray muzzle turned to the north. And then he whined. Had Dolores or Peter seen him or heard the note in his throat, they, too, would have stared back over the trail they had traveled. For something was coming to Wapi. Faint, elusive, and indefinable breath in the air, he smelled it in one moment, and the next it was gone. For many minutes he stood undecided, and then he returned to the sledge, his spine bristling and a growl in his throat.

Wide-eyed and staring, Peter was looking back. "What is it, Wapi?"

His voice aroused Dolores. She sat up with a start. The growl had grown into a snarl in Wapi's throat.

"I think they are coming," said Peter calmly. "You'd better rouse Uppy. He hasn't moved in the last two hours."

Something that was like a sob came from Dolores' lips as she stood up. "They're not coming," she whispered. "They've stopped - and they're building a fire!"

Not more than a third of a mile away a point of yellow flame flared up in the night.

"Give me the revolver, Peter."

Peter gave it to her without a word. She went to Uppy, and at the touch of her foot he was out of his sleeping-bag, his moon-face staring at her. She pointed back to the fire. Her face was dead white. The revolver was pointed straight at Uppy's heart.

"If they come up with us, Uppy - you die!"

The Eskimo's narrow eyes widened. There was murder in this white woman's face, in the steadiness of her hand, and in her voice. If they came up with them - he would die! Swiftly he gathered up his sleeping-bag and placed it on the sledge. Then he roused the dogs, tangled in their traces. They rose to their feet, sleepy and ill-humored. One of them snapped at his hand. Another snarled viciously as he untwisted a trace. Then one of the yawning brutes caught the new smell in the air, the smell that Wapi had gathered when it was a mile farther off. He sniffed. He sat back on his haunches and sent forth a yelping howl to his comrades in the other team. In ten seconds the other five were howling with him, and scarcely had the tumult burst from their throats when there came a response from the fire half a mile away.

"My God!" gasped Peter, under his breath.

Dolores sprang to the gee-bar, and Uppy lashed his long whip until it cracked like a repeating rifle over the pack. The dogs responded and sped through the night. Behind them the pandemonium of dog voices in the other camp had ceased. Men had leaped into life. Fifteen dogs were straightening in the tandem trace of a single sledge.

Dolores laughed, a sobbing, broken laugh, that in itself

was a cry of despair. "Peter, if they come up with us, what shall we do?"

"If they overtake us," said Peter, "give me the revolver. It is fully loaded?"

"I have cartridges - "

For the first time she remembered that she had not filled the three empty chambers. Crooking her arm under the gee-bar, she fumbled in her pocket. The dogs, refreshed by their sleep and urged by Uppy's whip, were tearing off the first mile at a great speed. The trail ahead of them was level and hard again. Uppy knew they were on the edge of the big barren of the Lacs Delesse, and he cracked his whip just as the off runner of the sledge struck a hidden snow-blister. There was a sudden lurch, and in a vicious up-shoot of the gee-bar the revolver was knocked from Dolores' hand - and was gone. A shriek rose to her lips, but she stifled it before it was given voice. Until this minute she had not felt the terror of utter hopelessness upon her. Now it made her faint. The revolver had not only given her hope, but also a steadfast faith in herself. From the beginning she had made up her mind how she would use it in the end, even though a few moments before she had asked Peter what they would do.

Crumpled down on the sledge, she clung to Peter, and suddenly the inspiration came to her not to let him know what had happened. Her arms tightened about his shoulders, and she looked ahead over the backs of the wolfish pack, shivering as she thought of what Uppy would do could he guess her loss. But he was running now for his life, driven on by his fear of her unerring marksmanship - and Wapi. She looked over her shoulder. Wapi was there, a huge gray shadow twenty paces behind. And she thought she heard a shout!

Peter was speaking to her. "Blake's dogs are tired," he was saying. "They were just about to camp, and ours have had a rest. Perhaps - "

"We shall beat them!" she interrupted him. "See how fast we are going, Peter! It is splendid!"

A rifle-shot sounded behind them. It was not far away, and involuntarily she clutched him tighter. Peter reached up a hand.

"Give me the revolver, Dolores."

"No," she protested. "They are not going to over-take us."

"You must give me the revolver," he insisted.

"Peter, I can't. You understand, I can't. I must keep the revolver."

She looked back again. There was no doubt now. Their pursuers were drawing nearer. She heard a voice, the la-looing of running Eskimos, a faint shout which she knew was a white man's shout - and another rifle shot. Wapi was running nearer. He was almost at the tail of the sledge, and his red eyes were fixed on her as he ran.

"Wapi!" she cried. "Wapi!"

His jaws dropped agape. She could hear his panting response to her voice.

A third shot - over their heads sped a strange droning sound.

"Wapi," she almost screamed, "go back! Sick 'em, Wapi - sick 'em - sick 'em - sick 'em!" She flung out her arms, driving him back, repeating the words over and over again. She leaned over the edge of the sledge, clinging to the gee-bar. "Go back, Wapi! Sick 'em - sick 'em - sick 'em!"

As if in response to her wild exhortation, there came a sudden yelping outcry from the team behind. It was close upon them now. Another ten minutes.

And then she saw that Wapi was dropping behind. Quickly he was swallowed up in the starlit chaos of the night.

"Peter," she cried, sobbingly. "Peter!"

Listening to the retreating sound of the sledge, Wapi stood a silent shadow in the trail. Then he turned and faced the north. He heard the other sound now, and ahead of it the wind brought him a smell, the smell of things he hated. For many years something had been fighting itself toward understanding within him, and the yelping of dogs and the taint in the air of creatures who had been his slave-masters narrowed his instinct to the one vital point. Again it was not a process of reason but the cumulative effect of things that had happened, and were happening. He had scented menace when first he had given warning of the nearness of pursuers, and this menace was no longer an elusive and unseizable thing that had merely stirred the fires of his hatred. It was now a near and physical fact. He had tried to run away from it - with the woman - but it had followed and was overtaking him, and the yelping dogs were challenging him to fight as they had challenged him from the day he was old enough to take his own part. And now he had something to fight for. His intelligence gripped the fact that one sledge was running away from the other, and that the sledge which was running away was his sledge - and that for his sledge he must fight.

He waited, almost squarely in the trail. There was no longer the slinking, club-driven attitude of a creature at bay in the manner in which he stood in the path of his enemies. He had risen out of his serfdom. The stinging slash of the whip and his dread of it were gone. Standing there in the starlight with his magnificent head thrown up and the muscles of his huge body like corded steel, the passing spirit of Shan Tung would have taken him for Tao, the Great Dane. He was not excited - and yet he was filled with a mighty desire - more than that, a tremendous purpose. The yelping excitement of the oncoming Eskimo dogs no longer urged him to turn aside to avoid their insolent bluster, as he would have turned aside yesterday or the day before. The voices of his old masters no longer sent him slinking out of their way, a growl in his throat and his body sagging with humiliation and the rage of his slavery. He stood like a rock, his broad chest facing them squarely, and when he saw the shadows of them racing up out of the star-mist an eighth of a mile away, it was not a growl but a whine that rose in his throat, a whine of low and repressed eagerness, of a great yearning about to be fulfilled. Two hundred yards - a hundred - eighty - not until the dogs were less than fifty from him did he move. And then, like a rock hurled by a mighty force, he was at them.

He met the onrushing weight of the pack breast to breast. There was no warning. Neither men nor dogs had seen the waiting shadow. The crash sent the lead-dog back with Wapi's great fangs in his throat, and in an instant the fourteen dogs behind had piled over them, tangled in their traces, yelping and snarling and biting, while over them round-faced, hooded men shouted shrilly and struck with their whips, and from the sledge a white man sprang with a rifle in his hands. It was Rydal. Under the mass of dogs Wapi, the Walrus, heard nothing of the shouts of men. He was fighting. He was fighting as he had never fought before in all the days of his life. The fierce little Eskimo dogs had smelled him, and they knew their enemy. The lead-dog was dead. A second Wapi had disemboweled with a single slash of his inch-long fangs. He was buried now. But his jaws met flesh and bone, and out of the squirming mass there rose fearful cries of agony that mingled hideously with the bawling of men and the snarling and yelping of beasts that had not yet felt Wapi's fangs. Three and four at a time they were at him. He felt the wolfish slash of their teeth in his flesh. In him the sense of pain was gone. His jaws closed on a foreleg, and it snapped like a stick. His teeth sank like ivory knives into the groin of a brute that had torn a hole in his side, and a smothered death-howl rose out of the heap. A fang pierced his eye. Even then no cry came from Wapi, the Walrus. He heaved upward with his giant body. He found another throat, and it was then that he rose above the pack, shaking the life from his victim as a terrier would have shaken a rat. For the first time the Eskimos saw him, and out of their superstitious souls strange cries found utterance as they sprang back and shrieked out to Rydal that it was a devil and not a beast that had waited for them in the trail. Rydal threw up his rifle. The shot came. It burned a crease in Wapi's shoulder and tore a hole as big as a man's fist in the breast of a dog about to spring upon him f rom behind. Again he was down, and Rydal dropped his rifle, and snatched a whip from the hand of an Eskimo. Shouting and cursing, he lashed the pack, and in a moment he saw a huge, open-jawed shadow rise up on the far side and start off into the open starlight. He sprang back to his rifle. Twice he fired at the retreating shadow before it disappeared. And the Eskimo dogs made no movement to follow. Five of the fifteen were dead. The remaining ten, torn and bleeding - three of them with legs that dragged in the bloody snow - gathered in a whipped and whimpering group. And the Eskimos, shivering in their fear of this devil that had entered into the body of Wapi, the Walrus, failed to respond to Rydal's command when he pointed to the red trail that ran out under the stars.

At Fort Confidence, one hundred and fifty miles to the south, there was day - day that was like cold, gray dawn, the day one finds just beyond the edge of the Arctic night, in which the sun hangs like a pale lantern over the far southern horizon. In a log-built room that faced this bit of glorious red glow lay Peter, bolstered up in his bed so that he could see it until it faded from the sky. There was a new light in his face, and there was something of the old Peter back in his eyes. Watching the final glow with him was Dolores. It was their second day.

Into this world, in the twilight that was falling swiftly as they watched the setting of the sun, came Wapi, the Walrus. Blinded in the eye, gaunt with hunger and exhaustion, covered with wounds, and with his great heart almost ready to die, he came at last to the river across which lay the barracks. His vision was nearly gone, but under his nose he could still smell faintly the trail he was following until the last. It led him across the river. And in darkness it brought him to a door.

After a little the door opened, and with its opening came at last the fulfilment of the promise of his dreams - hope, happiness, things to live for in a new, a white-man's world. For Wapi, the Walrus, forty years removed from Tao of Vancouver, had at last come home.

THE YELLOW-BACK

Above God's Lake, where the Bent Arrow runs red as pale blood under its crust of ice, Reese Beaudin heard of the dog auction that was to take place at Post Lac Bain three days later. It was in the cabin of Joe Delesse , a trapper, who lived at Lac Bain during the summer , and trapped the fox and the lynx sixty miles farther north in this month of February.

"Diantre, but I tell you it is to be the greatest sale of dogs that has ever happened at Lac Bain!" said Delesse. "To this Wakao they are coming from all the four directions. There will be a hundred dogs, huskies, and malamutes, and Mackenzie hounds, and mongrels from the south, and I should not wonder if some of the little Eskimo devils were brought from the north to be sold as breeders. Surely you will not miss it , my friend?"

"I am going by way of Post Lac Bain," replied Reese Beaudin equivocally.

But his mind was not on the sale of dogs. From his pipe he puffed out thick clouds of smoke, and his eyes narrowed until they seemed like coals peering out of cracks; and he said, in his quiet, soft voice:

"Do you know of a man named Jacques Dupont, m'sieu?"

Joe Delesse tried to peer through the cloud of smoke at Reese Beaudin's face.

"Yes, I know him. Does he happen to be a friend of yours?"

Reese laughed softly.

"I have heard of him. They say that he is a devil. To the west I was told that he can whip any man between Hudson's Bay and the Great Bear, that he is a beast in man-shape, and that he will surely be at the big sale at Lac Bain."

On his knees the huge hands of Joe Delesse clenched slowly, gripping in their imaginary clutch a hated thing.

"Oui, I know him," he said. "I know also - Elise - his wife. See!"

He thrust suddenly his two huge knotted hands through the smoke that drifted between him and the stranger who had sought the shelter of his cabin that night.

"See - I am a man full-grown, m'sieu - a man - and yet I am afraid of him! That is how much of a devil and a beast in man-shape he is."

Again Reese Beaudin laughed in his low, soft voice.

"And his wife, mon ami? Is she afraid of him?"

He had stopped smoking. Joe Delesse saw his face. The stranger's eyes made him look twice and think twice.

"You have known her - sometime?"

"Yes, a long time ago. "We were children together. And I have heard all has not gone well with her. Is it so?"

"Does it go well when a dove is mated to a vulture, m'sieu?"

"I have also heard that she grew up to be very beautiful," said Reese Beaudin, "and that Jacques Dupont killed a man for her. If that is so - "

"It is not so," interrupted Delesse. "He drove another man away - no, not a man, but a yellow-livered coward who had no more fight in him than a porcupine without quills! And yet she says he was not a coward. She has always said, even to Dupont, that it was the way le Bon Dieu made him, and that because he was made that way he was greater than all other men in the North Country. How do I know? Because, m'sieu, I am Elise Dupont's cousin."

Delesse wondered why Reese Beaudin's eyes were glowing like living coals.

"And yet - again, it is only rumor I have heard - they say this man, whoever he was, did actually run away, like a dog that had been whipped and was afraid to return to its kennel."

" Pst ! " Joe Delesse flung his great arms wide. "Like

that - he was gone. And no one ever saw him again, or heard of him again. But I know that she knew - my cousin, Elise. What word it was he left for her at the last she has always kept in her own heart, mon Dieu, and what a wonderful thing he had to fight for! You knew the child. But the woman - non? She was like an angel. Her eyes, when you looked into them - hat can I say, m'sieu? They made you forget. And I have seen her hair, unbound, black and glossy as the velvet side of a sable, covering her to the hips. And two years ago I saw Jacques Dupont's hands in that hair, and he was dragging her by it - "

Something snapped. It was a muscle in Reese Beaudin's arm. He had stiffened like iron.

"And you let him do that!"

Joe Delesse shrugged his shoulders. It was a shrug of hopelessness, of disgust.

"For the third time I interfered, and for the third time Jacques Dupont beat me until I was nearer dead than alive. And since then I have made it none of my business. It was, after all, the fault of the man who ran away. You see, m'sieu, it was like this: Dupont was mad for her, and this man who ran away - the Yellow-back - wanted her, and Elise loved the Yellow-back. This Yellow-back was twenty-three or four, and he read books, and played a fiddle and drew strange pictures - and was weak in the heart when it came to a fight. But Elise loved him. She loved him for those very things that made him a fool and a weakling, m'sieu, the books and the fiddle and the pictures; and she stood up with the courage for them both. And she would have married him, too, and would have fought for him with a club if it had come to that, when the thing happened that made him run away. It was at the midsummer carnival, when all the trappers and their wives and children were at Lac Bain. And Dupont followed the Yellow-back about like a dog. He taunted him, he insulted him, he got down on his knees and offered to fight him without getting on his feet; and there, before the very eyes of Elise, he washed the Yellow-back's face in the grease of one of the roasted caribou! And the Yellow-back was a man! Yes, a grown man! And it was then that Jacques Dupont shouted out his challenge to all that crowd. He would fight the Yellow-back. He would fight him with his right arm tied behind his back! And before Elise and the Yellow-back, and all that crowd, friends tied his arm so that it was like a piece of wood behind him, and it was his right arm, his fighting arm, the better half of him that was gone. And even then the Yellow-back was as white as the paper he drew pictures on. Ventre saint gris, but then was his chance to have killed Jacques Dupont! Half a man could have done it. Did he, m'sieu? No, he did not. With his one arm and his one hand Jacques Dupont whipped that Yellow-back, and he would have killed him if Elise had not rushed in to sav e the Yellow-back's purple face from going dead black. And that night the Yellow-back slunk away. Shame? Yes. From that night he was ashamed to show his face ever again at Lac Bain. And no one knows where he went. No one - except Elise. And her secret is in her own breast."

"And after that?" questioned Reese Beaudin, in a voice that was scarcely above a whisper.

"I cannot understand," said Joe Delesse. "It was strange, m'sieu, very strange. I know that Elise, even after that coward ran away, still loved him. And yet - well, something happened. I overheard a terrible quarrel one day between Jan Thiebout, father of Elise, and Jacques Dupont. After that Thiebout was very much afraid of Dupont. I have my own suspicion. Now that Thiebout is dead it is not wrong for me to say what it is. I think Thiebout killed the halfbreed Bedore who was found dead on his trap-line five years ago. There was a feud between them. And Dupont, discovering Thiebout's secret - well, you can understand how easy it would be after that, m'sieu. Thiebout's winter trapping was in that Burntwood country, fifty miles from neighbor to neighbor, and very soon after Bedore's death Jacques Dupont became Thiebout's partner. I know that Elise was forced to marry him. That was four years ago. The next year old Thiebout died, and in all that time not once has Elise been to Post Lac Bain!"

"Like the Yellow-back - she never returned," breathed Reese Beaudin.

"Never. And now - it is strange - "

"What is strange, Joe Delesse?"

"That for the first time in all these years she is going to Lac Bain - to the dog sale."

Reese Beaudin's face was again hidden in the smoke of his pipe. Through it his voice came.

"It is a cold night, M'sieu Delesse. Hear the wind howl!"

" Yes , it is cold - so cold the foxes will not run. My

traps and poison-baits will need no tending tomorrow."

"Unless you dig them out of the drifts."

"I will stay in the cabin."

"What! You are not going to Lac Bain!"

"I doubt it."

"Even though Elise, your cousin, is to be there?"

"I have no stomach for it, m'sieu. Nor would you were you in my boots, and did you know why he is going. Par les mille cornes d'u diable, I cannot whip him but I can kill him - and if I went - and the thing happens which I guess is going to happen - "

"Qui? Surely you will tell me - "

" Yes , I will tell you. Jacques Dupont knows that Elise has never stopped loving the Yellow-back. I do not believe she has ever tried to hide it from him. Why should she ? And there is a rumor , m'sieu, that the Yellow-back will be at the Lac Bain dog sale."

Reese Beaudin rose slowly to his feet, and yawned in that smoke-filled cabin.

"And if the Yellow-back should turn the tables, Joe Delesse, think of what a fine thing you will miss," he said.

Joe Delesse also rose, with a contemptuous laugh.

"That fiddler, that picture-drawer, that book-reader - Pouff! You are tired, m'sieu, that is your bunk."

Reese Beaudin held out a hand. The bulk of the two stood out in the lamp-glow, and Joe Delesse was so much the bigger man that his hand was half again the size of Reese Beaudin's. They gripped. And then a strange look went over the face of Joe Delesse. A cry came from out of his beard. His mouth grew twisted. His knees doubled slowly under him, and in the space of ten seconds his huge bulk was kneeling on the floor, while Reese Beaudin looked at him, smiling.

"Has Jacques Dupont a greater grip than that, Joe Delesse?" he asked in a voice that was so soft it was almost a woman's.

"Mon Dieu!" gasped Delesse. He staggered to his feet, clutching his crushed hand. "M'sieu - "

Reese Beaudin put his hands to the other's shoulders, smiling, friendly.

"I will apologize, I will explain, mon ami," he said. "But first, you must tell me the name of that Yellow-back who ran away years ago. Do you remember it?"

"Oui, but what has that to do with my crushed hand? The Yellow-back's name was Reese Beaudin - "

"And I am Reese Beaudin," laughed the other gently.

On that day - the day of Wakoa, the dog sale - seven fat caribou were roasting on great spits at Post Lac Bain, and under them were seven fires burning red and hot of seasoned birch, and around the seven fires were seven groups of men who slowly turned the roasting carcasses.

It was the Big Day of the mid-winter festival, and Post Lac Bain, with a population of twenty in times of quiet, was a seething wilderness metropolis of two hundred excited souls and twice as many dogs. From all directions they had come, from north and south and east and west; from near and from far, from the Barrens, from the swamps, from the farther forests, from river and lake and hidden trail - a few white men, mostly French; half-breeds and 'breeds, Chippewans, and Crees, and here and there a strange, dark-visaged little interloper from the north with his strain of Eskimo blood. Foregathered were all the breeds and creeds and fashions of the wilderness.

Over all this, pervading the air like an incense, stirring the desire of man and beast, floated the aroma of the roasting caribou. The feast-hour was at hand. With cries that rose above the last words of a wild song the seven groups of men rushed to seven pairs of props and tore them away. The great carcasses swayed in mid-air, bent slowly over their spits, and then crashed into the snow fifteen feet from the fire. About each carcass five men with razor-sharp knives ripped off hunks of the roasted flesh and passed them into eager hands of the hungry multitude. First came the women and children, and last the men.

On this there peered forth from a window in the factor's house the darkly bearded, smiling face of Reese Beaudin.

"I have seen him three times, wandering about in the crowd , seeking someone," he said. "Bien, he shall find that someone very soon!"

In the face of McDougall, the factor, was a strange look. For he had listened to a strange story, and there was still something of shock and amazement and disbelief in his eyes.

"Reese Beaudin, it is hard for me to believe."

"And yet you shall find that it is true," smiled Reese.

"He will kill you. He is a monster - a giant!"

"I shall die hard," replied Reese.

He turned from the window again, and took from the table a violin wrapped in buckskin, and softly he played one of their old love songs. It was not much more than a whisper, and yet it was filled with a joyous exultation. He laid the violin down when he was finished, and laughed, and filled his pipe, and lighted it.

"It is good for a man's soul to know that a woman loves him, and has been true," he said. "Mon pere, will you tell me again what she said? It is strength for me - and I must soon be going."

McDougall repeated, as if under a strain from which he could not free himself:

"She came to me late last night, unknown to Dupont. She had received your message, and knew you were coming. And I tell you again that I saw something in her eyes which makes me afraid! She told me, then, that her father killed Bedore in a quarrel, and that she married Dupont to save him from the law - and kneeling there, with her hand on the cross at her breast, she swore that each day of her life she has let Dupont know that she hates him, and that she loves you, and that some day Reese Beaudin would return to avenge her. Yes, she told him that - I know it by what I saw in her eyes. With that cross clutched in her fingers she swore that she had suffered torture and shame, and that never a word of it had she whispered to a living soul, that she might turn the passion of Jacques Dupont's black heart into a great hatred. And today - Jacques Dupont will kill you!"

"I shall die hard," Reese repeated again.

He tucked the violin in its buckskin covering under his arm. From the table he took his cap and placed it on his head.

In a last effort McDougall sprang from his chair and caught the other's arm.

"Reese Beaudin - you are going to your death! As factor of Lac Bain - agent of justice under power of the Police - I forbid it!"

"So-o-o-o," spoke Reese Beaudin gently. "Mon pere - "

He unbuttoned his coat, which had remained buttoned. Under the coat was a heavy shirt; and the shirt he opened, smiling into the factor's eyes, and McDougall's face froze, and the breath was cut short on his lips.

"That!" he gasped.

Reese Beaudin nodded.

Then he opened the door and went out.

Joe Delesse had been watching the factor's house, and he worked his way slowly along the edge of the feasters so that he might casually come into the path of Reese Beaudin. And there was one other man who also had watched, and who came in the same direction. He was a stranger, tall, closely hooded, his mustached face an Indian bronze. No one had ever seen him at Lac Bain before, yet in the excitement of the carnival the fact passed without conjecture or significance. And from the cabin of Henri Paquette another pair of eyes saw Reese Beaudin, and Mother Paquette heard a sob that in itself was a prayer.

In and out among the devourers of caribou-flesh, scanning the groups and the ones and the twos and the threes, passed Jacques Dupont, and with him walked his friend, one-eyed Layonne. Layonne was a big man, but Dupont was taller by half a head. The brutishness of his face was hidden under a coarse red beard; but the devil in him glowered from his deep-set, inhuman eyes; it walked in his gait, in the hulk of his great shoulders, in the gorilla-like slouch of his hips. His huge hands hung partly clenched at his sides. His breath was heavy with whisky that Layonne himself had smuggled in, and in his heart was black murder.

"He has not come!" he cried for the twentieth time. "He has not come!"

He moved on, and Reese Beaudin - ten feet away - turned and smiled at Joe Delesse with triumph in his eyes. He moved nearer.

" Did I not tell you he would not find in me that

narrow-shouldered, smooth-faced stripling of five years ago?" he asked. "N'est-ce pas, friend Delesse?"

The face of Joe Delesse was heavy with a somber fear.

"His fist is like a wood-sledge, m'sieu."

"So it was years ago."

"His forearm is as big as the calf of your leg."

"Oui, friend Delesse, it is the forearm of a giant."

"He is half again your weight."

"Or more, friend Delesse."

"He will kill you! As the great God lives, he will kill you!"

"I shall die hard," repeated Reese Beaudin for the third time that day.

Joe Delesse turned slowly, doggedly. His voice rumbled.

"The sale is about to begin, m'sieu. See!"

A man had mounted the log platform raised to the height of a man's shoulders at the far end of the clearing. It was Henri Paquette, master of the day's ceremonies, and appointed auctioneer of the great wakao. A man of many tongues was Paquette. To his lips he raised a great megaphone of birchbark, and sonorously his call rang out - in French , in Cree , in Chippewan, and the packed throng about the caribou-fires heaved like a living billow, and to a man and a woman and a child it moved toward the appointed place.

"The time has come," said Reese Beaudin. "And all Lac Bain shall see!"

Behind them - watching, always watching - followed the bronze-faced stranger in his close-drawn hood.

For an hour the men of Lac Bain gathered close-wedged about the log platform on which stood Henri Paquette and his Indian helper. Behind the men were the women and children, and through the cordon there ran a babiche-roped pathway along which the dogs were brought.

The platform was twenty feet square, with the floor side of the logs hewn flat, and there was no lack of space for the gesticulation and wild pantomime of Paquette. In one hand he held a notebook, and in the other a pencil. In the notebook the sales of twenty dogs were already tabulated, and the prices paid.

Anxiously, Reese Beaudin was waiting. Each time that a new dog came up he looked at Joe Delesse, but, as yet Joe had failed to give the signal.

On the platform the Indian was holding two malamutes in leash now and Paquette was crying, in a well simulated fit of great fury:

"What, you cheap kimootisks, will you let this pair of malamutes go for seven mink and a cross fox. Are you men? Are you poverty-stricken? Are you blind? A breed dog and a male giant for seven mink and a cross fox? Non, I will buy them myself first, and kill them, and use their flesh for dog-feed, and their hides for fools' caps! I will - "

"Twelve mink and a Number Two Cross," came a voice out of the crowd.

"Twelve mink and a Number One," shouted another.

"A little better - a little better!" wailed Paquette. "You are waking up, but slowly - mon Dieu, so slowly! Twelve mink and - "

A voice rose in Cree:

"Nesi-tu-now-unisk!"

Paquette gave a triumphant yell.

"The Indian beats you! The Indian from Little Neck Lake - an Indian beats the white man! He offers twenty beaver - prime skins! And beaver are wanted in Paris now. They're wanted in London. Beaver and gold - they are the same! But they are the price of one dog alone. Shall they both go at that? Shall the Indian have them for twenty beaver - twenty beaver that may be taken from a single house in a day - while it has taken these malamutes two and a half years to grow? I say, you cheap kimootisks - "

And then an amazing thing happened. It was like a bomb falling in that crowded throng of wondering and amazed forest people.

It was the closely hooded stranger who spoke.

"I will give a hundred dollars cash," he said.

A look of annoyance crossed Reese Beaudin's face.

He was close to the bronze-faced stranger, and edged nearer.

"Let the Indian have them," he said in a low voice. "It is Meewe. I knew him years ago. He has carried me on his back. He taught me first to draw pictures."

"But they are powerful dogs," objected the stranger. "My team needs them."

The Cree had risen higher out of the crowd. One arm rose above his head. He was an Indian who had seen fifty years of the forests, and his face was the face of an Egyptian.

"Nesi-tu-now Nesoo-sap umisk!" he proclaimed.

Henri Paquette hopped excitedly, and faced the stranger.

"Twenty-two beaver," he challenged. "Twenty-two - "

"Let Meewe have them," replied the hooded stranger.

Three minutes later a single dog was pulled up on the log platform. He was a magnificent beast, and a rumble of approval ran through the crowd.

The face of Joe Delesse was gray. He wet his lips. Reese Beaudin, watching him, knew that the time had come. And Joe Delesse, seeing no way of escape, whispered:

"It is her dog, m'sieu. It is Parka - and Dupont sells him today to show her that he is master."

Already Paquette was advertising the virtues of Parka when Reese Beaudin, in a single leap, mounted the log platform, and stood beside him.

"Wait!" he cried.

There fell a silence, and Reese said, loud enough for all to hear:

"M'sieu Paquette, I ask the privilege of examining this dog that I want to buy."

At last he straightened, and all who faced him saw the smiling sneer on his lips.

"Who is it that offers this worthless cur for sale?" Lac Bain heard him say. "P-s-s-st - it is a woman's dog! It is not worth bidding for!"

"You lie!" Dupont's voice rose in a savage roar. His huge shoulders bulked over those about him. He crowded to the edge of the platform. "You lie!"

"He is a woman's dog," repeated Reese Beaudin without excitement, yet so clearly that every ear heard. "He is a woman's pet, and M'sieu Dupont most surely does lie if he denies it!"

So far as memory went back no man at Lac Bain that day had ever heard another man give Jacques Dupont the lie. A thrill swept those who heard and understood. There was a great silence, in that silence men near him heard the choking rage in Dupont's great chest. He was staring up - straight up into the smiling face of Reese Beaudin; and in that moment he saw beyond the glossy black beard, and amazement and unbelief held him still. In the next, Reese Beaudin had the violin in his hands. He flung off the buckskin, and in a flash the instrument was at his shoulder.

"See! I will play, and the woman's pet shall sing!"

And once more, after five years, Lac Bain listened to the magic of Reese Beaudin's violin. And it was Elise's old love song that he played. He played it, smiling down into the eyes of a monster whose face was turning from red to black; yet he did not play it to the end, nor a quarter of it, for suddenly a voice shouted:

"It is Reese Beaudin - come back!"

Joe Delesse, paralyzed, speechless, could have sworn it was the hooded stranger who shouted; and then he remembered, and flung up his great arms, and bellowed:

"Oui - by the Saints, it is Reese Beaudin - Reese Beaudin come back!"

Suddenly as it had begun the playing ceased, and Henri Paquette found himself with the violin in his hands. Reese Beaudin turned, facing them all, the wintry sun glowing in his beard, his eyes smiling, his head high - unfraid now, more fearless than any other man that had ever set foot in Lac Bain. And McDougall, with his arm touching Elise's hair, felt the wild and throbbing pulse of her body. This day - this hour - this minute in which she stood still, inbreathing - had confirmed her belief in Reese Beaudin. As she had dreamed, so had he risen. First of all the men in the world he stood there now, just as he had been first in the days when she had loved his dreams, his music, and his pictures. To her he was the old god, more splendid, - for he had risen above fear, and he was facing Dupont now with that strange quiet smile on his lips. And then, all at once, her soul broke its fetters, and over the women's heads she reached out her arms, and all there heard her voice in its triumph, its joy, its fear.

"Reese! Reese - my sakeakun!"

Over the heads of all the forest people she called him beloved! Like the fang of an adder the word stung Dupont's brain. And like fire touched to powder, swiftly as lightning illumines the sky, the glory of it blazed in Reese Beaudin's face. And all that were there heard him clearly:

"I am Reese Beaudin. I am the Yellow-back. I have returned to meet a man you all know - Jacques Dupont. He is a monkey-man - a whipper of boys, a stealer of women, a cheat, a coward, a thing so foul the crows will not touch him when he dies - "

There was a roar. It was not the roar of a man, but of a beast - and Jacques Dupont was on the platform!

Quick as Dupont's movement had been it was no swifter than that of the closely-hooded stranger. He was as tall as Dupont, and about him there was an air of authority and command.

"Wait," he said, and placed a hand on Dupont's heaving chest. His smile was cold as ice. Never had Dupont seen eyes so like the pale blue of steel.

"M'sieu Dupont, you are about to avenge a great insult. It must be done fairly. If you have weapons, throw them away. I will search this - this Reese Beaudin, as he calls himself! And if there is to be a fight, let it be a good one. Strip yourself to that great garment you have on, friend Dupont. See, our friend - this Reese Beaudin - is already stripping!"

He was unbuttoning the giant's heavy Hudson's Bay coat. He pulled it off, and drew Dupont's knife from its sheath. Paquette, like a stunned cat that had recovered its ninth life, was scrambling from the platform. The Indian was already gone. And Reese Beaudin had tossed his coat to Joe Delesse, and with it his cap. His heavy shirt was closely buttoned; and not only was it buttoned, Delesse observed, but also was it carefully pinned. And even now, facing that monster who would soon be at him, Reese Beaudin was smiling.

For a moment the closely hooded stranger stood between them, and Jacques Dupont crouched himself for his vengeance. Never to the people of Lac Bain had he looked more terrible. He was the gorilla-fighter, the beast fighter, the fighter who fights as the wolf, the bear and the cat - crushing out life, breaking bones, twisting, snapping, inundating and destroying with his great weight and his monstrous strength. He was a hundred pounds heavier than Reese Beaudin. On his stooping shoulders he could carry a tree. With his giant hands he could snap a two-inch sapling. With one hand alone he had set a bear-trap. And with that mighty strength he fought as the cave-man fought. It was his boast there was no trick of the Chippewan, the Cree, the Eskimo or the forest man that he did not know. And yet Reese Beaudin stood calmly, waiting for him, and smiling!

In another moment the hooded stranger was gone, and there was none between them.

"A long time I have waited for this, m'sieu," said Reese, for Dupont's ears alone. "Five years is a long time. And my Elise still loves me."

Still more like a gorilla Jacques Dupont crept upon him. His face was twisted by a rage to which he could no longer give voice. Hatred and jealousy robbed his eyes of the last spark of the thing that was human. His great hands were hooked, like an eagle's talons. His lips were drawn back, like a beast's. Through his red beard yellow fangs were bared.

And Reese Beaudin no longer smiled. He laughed!

"Until I went away and met real men, I never knew what a pig of a man you were, M'sieu Dupont," he taunted amiably, as though speaking in jest to a friend. "You remind me of an aged and over-fat porcupine with his big paunch and crooked arms. What horror must it have been for my Elise to have lived in sight of such a beast as you!"

With a bellow Dupont was at him. And swifter than eyes had ever seen man move at Lac Bain before, Reese Beaudin was out of his way, and behind him; and then , as the giant caught himself at the edge of the platform, and turned, he received a blow that sounded like the broadside of a paddle striking water. Reese Beaudin had struck him with the flat of his unclenched hand!

A murmur of incredulity rose out of the crowd. To the forest man such a blow was the deadliest of insults. It was calling him an Iskwao - a woman - a weakling - a thing too contemptible to harden one's fist against. But the murmur died in an instant. For Reese Beaudin, making as if to step back, shot suddenly forward - straight through the giant's crooked arms - and it was his fist this time that landed squarely between the eyes of Dupont. The monster's head went back, his great body wavered, and then suddenly he plunged backward off the platform and fell with a crash to the ground.

A yell went up from the hooded stranger. Joe Delesse split his throat. The crowd drowned Reese Beaudin's voice. But above it all rose a woman's voice shrieking forth a name.

And then Jacques Dupont was on the platform again. In the moments that followed one could almost hear his neighbor's heart beat. Nearer and still nearer to each other drew the two men. And now Dupont crouched still more, and Joe Delesse held his breath. He noticed that Reese Beaudin was standing almost on the tips of his toes - that each instant he seemed prepared, like a runner, for sudden flight. Five feet - four - and Dupont leapt in, his huge arms swinging like the limb of a tree, and his weight following with crushing force behind his blow. For an instant it seemed as though Reese Beaudin had stood to meet that fatal rush, but in that same instant - so swiftly that only the hooded stranger knew what had happened - he was out of the way, and his left arm seemed to shoot downward, and then up, and then his right straight out, and then again his left arm downward, and up - and it was the third blow, all swift as lightning, that brought a yell from the hooded stranger. For though none but the stranger had seen it, Jacques Dupont's head snapped back - and all saw the fourth blow that sent him reeling like a man struck by a club.

There was no sound now. A mental and a vocal paralysis seized upon the inhabitants of Lac Bain. Never had they seen fighting like this fighting of Reese Beaudin. Until now had they lived to see the science of the sawdust ring pitted against the brute force of Brobdingnagian, of Antaeus and Goliath. For Reese Beaudin's fighting was a fighting without tricks that they could see. He used his fists, and his fists alone. He was like a dancing man. And suddenly, in the midst of the miracle, they saw Jacques Dupont go down. And the second miracle was that Reese Beaudin did not leap on him when he had fallen. He stood back a little, balancing himself in that queer fashion on the balls and toes of his feet. But no sooner was Dupont up than Reese Beaudin was in again, with the swiftness of a cat, and they could hear the blows, like solid shots, and Dupont's arms waved like tree-tops, and a second time he was off the platform.

He was staggering when he rose. The blood ran in streams from his mouth and nose. His beard dripped with it. His yellow teeth were caved in.

This time he did not leap upon the platform - he clambered back to it, and the hooded stranger gave him a lift which a few minutes before Dupont would have resented as an insult.

"Ah, it has come," said the stranger to Delesse.

"He is the best close-in fighter in all - "

He did not finish.

"I could kill you now - kill you with a single blow," said Reese Beaudin in a moment when the giant stood swaying. "But there is a greater punishment in store for you, and so I shall let you live!"

And now Reese Beaudin was facing that part of the crowd where the woman he loved was standing. He was breathing deeply. But he was not winded. His eyes were black as night, his hair wind-blown. He looked straight over the heads between him and she whom Dupont had stolen from him.

Reese Beaudin raised his arms, and where there had been a murmur of voices there was now silence.

For the first time the stranger threw back his hood. He was unbuttoning his heavy coat.

And Joe Delesse, looking up, saw that Reese Beaudin was making a mighty effort to quiet a strange excitement within his breast. And then there was a rending of cloth and of buttons and of pins as in one swift movement he tore the shirt from his own breast - exposing to the eyes of Lac Bain blood-red in the glow of the winter sun, the crimson badge of the Royal Northwest Mounted Police!

And above the gasp that swept the multitude, above the strange cry of the woman, his voice rose:

"I am Reese Beaudin, the Yellow-back. I am Reese Beaudin, who ran away. I am Reese Beaudin, - Sergeant in His Majesty's Royal Northwest Mounted Police, and in the name of the law I arrest Jacques Dupont for the murder of Francois Bedore, who was killed on his trap-line five years ago! Fitzgerald - "

The hooded stranger leaped upon the platform. His heavy coat fell off. Tall and grim he stood in the scarlet jacket of the Police. Steel clinked in his hands. And Jacques Dupont, terror in his heart, was trying to see as he groped to his knees. The steel snapped over his wrists.

And then he heard a voice close over him. It was the voice of Reese Beaudin.

"And this is your final punishment, Jacques Dupont - to be hanged by the neck until you are dead. For Bedore was not dead when Elise's father left him after their fight on the trap-line. It was you who saw the fight, and finished the killing, and laid the crime on Elise's father. Mukoki, the Indian, saw you. It is my day, Dupont, and I have waited long - "

The rest Dupont did not hear. For up from the crowd there went a mighty roar. And through it a woman was making her way with outreaching arms - and behind her followed the factor of Lac Bain.

THE FIDDLING MAN

Breault's cough was not pleasant to hear. A cough possesses manifold and almost unclassifiable diversities. But there is only one cough when a man has a bullet through his lungs and is measuring his life by minutes, perhaps seconds. Yet Breault, even as he coughed the red stain from his lips, was not afraid. Many times he had found himself in the presence of death, and long ago it had ceased to frighten him. Some day he had expected to come under the black shadow of it himself - not in a quiet and peaceful way, but all at once, with a shock. And the time had come. He knew that he was dying; and he was calm. More than that - in dying he was achieving a triumph. The red-hot death-sting in his lung had given birth to a frightful thought in his sickening brain. The day of his great opportunity was at hand. The hour - the minute.

A last flush of the pale afternoon sun lighted up his black-bearded face as his eyes turned, with their new inspiration, to his sledge. It was a face that one would remember - not pleasantly, perhaps, but as a fixture in a shifting memory of things; a face strong with a brute strength, implacable in its hard lines, emotionless almost, and beyond that, a mystery.

It was the best known face in all that part of the northland which reaches up from Fort McMurray to

Lake Athabasca and westward to Fond du Lac and the Wholdais country. For ten years Breault had made that trip twice a year with the northern mails. In all its reaches there was not a cabin he did not know, a face he had not seen, or a name he could not speak; yet there was not a man, woman, or child who welcomed him except for what he brought. But the government had found its faith in him justified. The police at their lonely outposts had come to regard his comings and goings as dependable as day and night. They blessed him for his punctuality, and not one of them missed him when he was gone. A strange man was Breault.

With his back against a tree, where he had propped himself after the first shock of the bullet in his lung, he took a last look at life with a passionless imperturbability. If there was any emotion at all in his face it was one of vindictiveness - an emotion roused by an intense and terrible hatred that in this hour saw the fulfilment of its vengeance. Few men nursed a hatred as Breault had nursed his. And it gave him strength now, when another man would have died.

He measured the distance between himself and the sledge. It was, perhaps, a dozen paces. The dogs were still standing, tangled a little in their traces, - eight of them, - wide-chested, thin at the groins, a wolfish horde, built for endurance and speed. On the sledge was a quarter of a ton of his Majesty's mail. Toward this Breault began to creep slowly and with great pain. A hand inside of him seemed crushing the fiber of his lung, so that the blood oozed out of his mouth. When he reached the sledge there were many red patches in the snow behind him. He opened with considerable difficulty a small dunnage sack, and after fumbling a bit took there-from a pencil attached to a long red string, and a soiled envelope.

For the first time a change came upon his countenance - a ghastly smile. And above his hissing breath, that gushed between his lips with the sound of air pumped through the fine mesh of a colander, there rose a still more ghastly croak of exultation and of triumph. Laboriously he wrote. A few words, and the pencil dropped from his stiffening fingers into the snow. Around his neck he wore a long red scarf held together by a big brass pin, and to this pin he fastened securely the envelope.

This much done, - the mystery of his death solved for those who might some day find him, - the ordinary man would have contented himself by yielding up life's struggle with as little more physical difficulty as possible. Breault was not ordinary. He was, in his one way, efficiency incarnate. He made space for himself on the sledge, and laid himself out in that space with great care, first taking pains to fasten about his thighs two babiche thongs that were employed at times to steady his freight. Then he ran his left arm through one of the loops of the stout mail-chest. By taking these precautions he was fairly secure in the belief that after he was dead and frozen stiff no amount of rough trailing by the dogs could roll him from the sledge.

In this conjecture he was right. When the starved and exhausted malamutes dragged their silent burden into the Northwest Mounted Police outpost barracks at Crooked Bow twenty-four hours later, an ax and a sapling bar were required to pry Francois Breault from his bier. Previous to this process, however, Sergeant Fitzgerald, in charge at the outpost, took possession of the soiled envelope pinned to Breault's red scarf. The information it bore was simple, and yet exceedingly definite. Few men in dying as Breault had died could have made the matter easier for the police.

On the envelope he had written:

Jan Thoreau shot me and left me for dead. Have just strength to write this - no more.

Francois Breault.

It was epic - a colossal monument to this man, thought Sergeant Fitzgerald, as they pried the frozen body loose.

To Corporal Blake fell the unpleasant task of going after Jan Thoreau. Unpleasant, because Breault's starved huskies and frozen body brought with them the worst storm of the winter. In the face of this storm Blake set out, with the Sergeant's last admonition in his ears:

"Don't come back, Blake, until you've got him, dead or alive."

That is a simple and efficacious formula in the rank and file of the Royal Northwest Mounted Police. It has made volumes of stirring history, because it means a great deal and has been lived up to. Twice before, the words had been uttered to Blake - in extreme cases. The first time they had taken him for six months into the Barren Lands between Hudson's Bay and the Great Slave - and he came back with his man; the second time he was gone for nearly a year along the rim of the Arctic - and from there also he came back with his man. Blake was of that sort. A bull-dog, a Nemesis when he was once on the trail, and - like most men of that kind - without a conscience. In the Blue Books of the service he was credited with arduous patrols and unusual exploits. "Put Blake on the trail" meant something, and "He is one of our best men" was a firmly established conviction at departmental headquarters.

Only one man knew Blake as Blake actually lived under his skin - and that was Blake himself. He hunted men and ran them down without mercy - not because he loved the law, but for the reason that he had in him the inherited instincts of the hound. This comparison, if quite true, is none the less unfair to the hound. A hound is a good dog at heart.

In the January storm it may be that the vengeful spirit of Francois Breault set out in company with Corporal Blake to witness the consummation of his vengeance. That first night, as he sat close to his fire in the shelter of a thick spruce timber, Blake felt the unusual and disturbing sensation of a presence somewhere near him. The storm was at its height. He had passed through many storms, but to-night there seemed to be an uncannily concentrated fury in its beating and wailing over the roofs of the forests.

He was physically comfortable. The spruce trees were so dense that the storm did not reach him, and fortune favored him with a good fire and plenty of fuel. But the sensation oppressed him. He could not keep away from him his mental vision of Breault as he had helped to pry him from the sledge - his frozen features, the stiffened fingers, the curious twist of the icy lips that had been almost a grin.

Blake was not superstitious. He was too much a man of iron for that. His soul had lost the plasticity of imagination. But he could not forget Breault's lips as they had seemed to grin up at him. There was a reason for it. On his last trip down, Breault had said to him, with that same half-grin on his face:

"M'sieu, some day you may go after my murderer, and when you do, Francois Breault will go with you."

That was three months ago. Blake measured the time back as he sucked at his pipe, and at the same time he looked at the shadowy and half-lost forms of his dogs, curled up for the night in the outer rim of firelight.

Over the tree-tops a sudden blast of wind howled. It was like a monster voice. Blake rose to his feet and rolled upon the fire the big night log he had dragged in, and to this he added, with the woodman's craft of long experience, lengths of green timber, so arranged that they would hold fire until morning. Then he went into his silk service tent and buried himself in his sleeping-bag.

For a long time he did not sleep. He listened to the crackle of the fire. Again and again he heard that monster voice moaning and shrieking over the forest. Never had the rage of storm filled him with the uneasiness of to-night. At last the mystery of it was solved for him. The wind came and went each time in a great moaning, half shrieking sound: B-r-r-r-r - e-e-e-e - aw-w-w-w!

It was like a shock to him; and yet, he was not a superstitious man. No, he was not that. He would have staked his life on it. But it was not pleasant to hear a dead man's name shrieked over one's head by the wind. Under the cover of his sleeping-bag flap Corporal Blake laughed. Funny things were always happening, he tried to tell himself. And this was a mighty good joke. Breault wasn't so slow, after all. He had given his promise, and he was keeping it; for, if it wasn't really Breault's voice up there in the wind, multiplied a thousand times, it was a good imitation of it. Again Corporal Blake laughed - a laugh as unpleasant as the cough that had come from Breault's bullet-punctured lung. He fell asleep after a time; but even sleep could not drive from him the clinging obsession of the thought that strange things were to happen in this taking of Jan Thoreau.

With the gray dawn there was nothing to mark the passing of the storm except freshly fallen snow, and Blake was on the trail before it was light enough to see a hundred yards ahead. There was a defiance and a contempt of last night in the crack of his long caribou-gut whip and the halloo of his voice as he urged on his dogs. Breault's voice in the wind? Bah! Only a fool would have thought that. Therefore he was a fool. And Jan Thoreau - it would be like taking a child. There would be no happenings to report - merely an arrest, a quick return journey, an affair altogether too ordinary to be interesting. Perhaps it was all on account of the hearty supper of caribou liver he had eaten. He was fond of liver, and once or twice before it had played him tricks.

He began to wonder if he would find Jan Thoreau at home. He remembered Jan quite vividly. The Indians called him Kitoochikun because he played a fiddle. Blake, the Iron Man, disliked him because of that fiddle. Jan was never without it, on the trail or off. The

Fiddling Man, he called him contemptuously - a baby, a woman; not fit for the big north. Tall and slim, with blond hair in spite of his French blood and name, a quiet and unexcitable face, and an air that Blake called "damned superiority." He wondered how the Fiddling Man had ever screwed up nerve enough to kill Breault. Undoubtedly there had been no fight. A quick and treacherous shot, no doubt. That was like a man who played a fiddle. POOF! He had no more respect for him than if he dressed in woman's clothing.

And he DID have a wife, this Jan Thoreau. They lived a good twenty miles off the north-and-south trail, on an island in the middle of Black Bear Lake. He had never seen the wife. A poor sort of woman, he made up his mind, that would marry a fiddler. Probably a half-breed; maybe an Indian. Anyway, he had no sympathy for her. Without a doubt, it was the woman who did the trapping and cut the wood. Any man who would tote a fiddle around on his back -

Corporal Blake traveled fast, and it was afternoon of the second day when he came to the dense spruce forest that shut in Black Bear Lake. Here something happened to change his plans somewhat. He met an Indian he knew - an Indian who, for two or three good reasons that stuck in the back of his head, dared not lie to him; and this tribesman, coming straight from the Thoreau cabin, told him that Jan was not at home, but had gone on a three-day trip to see the French missioner who lived on one of the lower Wholdaia waterways.

Blake was keen on strategem. With him, man-hunting was like a game of chess; and after he had questioned the Indian for a quarter of an hour he saw his opportunity. Pastamoo, the Cree, was made a part of his Majesty's service on the spot, with the promise of torture and speedy execution if he proved himself a traitor.

Blake turned over to him his dogs and sledge, his provisions, and his tent, and commanded him to camp in the heart of a cedar swamp a few miles back, with the information that he would return for his outfit at some time in the indefinite future. He might be gone a day or a week. When he had seen Pastamoo off, he continued his journey toward the cabin, in the hope that Jan Thoreau's wife was either an Indian or a fool. He was too old a hand at his game to be taken in by the story that had been told to the Cree.

Jan had not gone to the French missioner's. A murderer's trail would not be given away like that. Of course the wife knew. And Corporal Blake desired no better string to a criminal than the faith of a wife. Wives were easy if handled right, and they had put the finishing touch to more than one of his great successes.

At the edge of the lake he fell back on his old trick - hunger, exhaustion, a sprained leg. It was not more than a quarter of a mile across the snow-covered ice of the lake to the thin spiral of smoke that he saw rising above the thick balsams on the island. Five times in that distance he fell upon his face; he crawled like a man about to die. He performed an arduous task, a devilish task, and when at last he reached the balsams he cursed his luck until he was red in the face. No one had seen him. That quarter-mile of labor was lost, its finesse a failure. But he kept up the play, and staggered weakly through the sheltering balsams to the cabin. His artifice had no shame, even when played on women;

and he fell heavily against the door, beat upon it with his fist; and slipped down into the snow, where he lay with his head bowed, as if his last strength was gone.

He heard movement inside, quick steps - and then the door opened. He did not look up for a moment. That would have been crude. When he did raise his head, it was very slowly, with a look of anguish in his face. And then - he stared. His body all at once grew tense, and the counterfeit pain in his eyes died out like a flash in this most astounding moment of his life. Man of iron though he was, steeled to the core against the weaknesses of sudden emotions , it was impossible for him to restrain the gasp of amazement that rose to his lips.

In that stifled cry Jan Thoreau's wife heard the supplication of a dying man. She did not catch, back of it, the note of a startled beast. She was herself startled, frightened for a moment by the unexpectedness of it all.

And Blake stared. This - the fiddler's wife! She was clutching in her hand a brush with which she had been arranging her hair. The hair, jet black, was wonderful. Her eyes were still more wonderful to Blake. She was not an Indian - not a half-breed - and beautiful. The loveliest face he had ever visioned, sleeping or awake, was looking down at him.

With a second gasp, he remembered himself, and his body sagged, and the amazed stare went out of his eyes as he allowed his head to fall a little. In this movement his cap fell off. In another moment she was at his side, kneeling in the snow and bending over him.

"You are hurt, m'sieu!"

Her hair fell upon him, smothering his neck and shoulders. The perfume of it was like the delicate scent of a rare flower in his nostrils. A strange thrill swept through him. He did not try to analyze it in those few astonishing moments. It was beyond his comprehension, even had he tried. He was ignorant of the finer fundamentals of life, and of the great truth that the case-hardened nature of a man, like the body of an athlete, crumbles fastest under sudden and unexpected change and strain.

He regained his feet slowly and stupidly, assisted by Marie. They climbed the one step to the door. As he sank back heavily on the cot, in the room they entered, a thick tress of her hair fell softly upon his face. He closed his eyes for a space. When he opened them, Marie was bending over the stove.

And SHE was Thoreau's wife! The instant he had looked up into her face, he had forgotten the fiddler; but he remembered him now as he watched the woman, who stood with her back toward him. She was as slim as a reed. Her hair fell to her hips. He drew a deep breath. Unconsciously he clenched his hands. SHE - the fiddler's wife! The thought repeated itself again and again. Jan Thoreau, MURDERER, and this woman - HIS WIFE.

She returned in a moment with hot tea, and he drank with subtle hypocrisy from the cup she held to his lips.

"Sprained my leg," he said then, remembering his old part, and replying to the questioning anxiety in her eyes. " Dogs ran away and left me, and I got here just by chance. A little more and - "

He smiled grimly, and as he sank back he gave a sharp cry. He had practised that cry in more than one cabin, and along with it a convulsion of his features to emphasize the impression he labored to make.

"I'm afraid - I'll be a trouble to you," he apologized. "It's not broken; but it's bad, and I won't be able to move - soon. Is Jan at home?"

"No, m'sieu; he is away."

"Away," repeated Blake disappointedly. "Perhaps sometime he has told you about me," he added with sudden hopefulness. "I am John Duval."

"M'sieu - DUVAL!"

Marie's eyes, looking down at him, became all at once great pools of glowing light. Her lips parted. She leaned toward him, her slim hands clasped suddenly to her breast.

"M'sieu Duval - who nursed him through the smallpox?" she cried, her voice trembling. "M'sieu Duval - who saved my Jan's life!"

Blake had looked up his facts at headquarters. He knew what Duval, the Barren Land trapper, had once upon a time done for Jan.

"Yes; I am John Duval," said. "And so - you see - I am sorry that Jan is away."

" But he is coming back soon - in a few days , "

exclaimed Marie. "You shall stay, m'sieu! You will wait for him? Yes?"

"This leg - " began Blake. He cut himself short with a grimace. "Yes, I'll stay. I guess I'll have to."

Marie had changed at the mention of Duval's name. With the glow in her eyes had come a flush into her cheeks, and Blake could see the strange little quiver at her throat as she looked at him. But she did not see Blake so much as what lay beyond him - Duval's lonely cabin away up on the edge of the Great Barren, the hours of darkness and agony through which Jan had passed, and the magnificent comradeship of this man who had now dragged himself to their own cabin, half dead.

Many times Jan had told her the story of that terrible winter when Duval had nursed him like a woman, and had almost given up his life as a sacrifice. And this - THIS - was Duval? She bent over him again as he lay on the cot, her eyes shining like stars in the growing dusk. In that dusk she was unconscious of the fact that his fingers had found a long tress of her hair and were clutching it passionately. Remembering Duval as Jan had enshrined him in her heart, she said:

"I have prayed many times that the great God might thank you, m'sieu."

He raised a hand. For an instant it touched her soft, warm cheek and caressed her hair. Marie did not shrink - yes, that would have been an insult. Even Jan would have said that. For was not this Duval, to whom she owed all the happiness in her life - Duval, more than brother to Jan Thoreau, her husband?

"And you - are Marie?" said Blake.

"Yes, m'sieu, I am Marie."

A joyous note trembled in her voice as she drew back from the cot. He could hear her swiftly braiding her hair before she struck a match to light the oil lamp hanging from the ceiling. After that, through partly closed eyes, he watched her as she prepared their supper. Occasionally, when she turned toward him as if to speak, he feigned a desire to sleep. It was a catlike watchfulness, filled with his old cunning. In his face there was no sign to betray its hideous significance. Outwardly he had regained his iron-like impassiveness; but in his body and his brain every nerve and fiber was consumed by a monstrous desire - a desire for this woman, the murderer's wife. It was as strange and as sudden as the death that had come to Francois Breault.

The moment he had looked up into her face in the doorway, it had overwhelmed him. And now even the sound of her footsteps on the floor filled him with an exquisite exultation. It was more than exultation. It was a feeling of POSSESSION.

In the hollow of his hand he - Blake, the man-hunter - held the fate of this woman. She was the Fiddler's wife - and the Fiddler was a murderer.

Marie heard the sudden deep breath that forced itself from his lips, a gasp that would have been a cry of triumph if he had given it voice.

"You are in pain, m'sieu," she exclaimed, turning toward him quickly.

"A little," he said, smiling at her. "Will you help me to sit up, Marie?"

He saw ahead of him another and more thrilling game than the man-hunt now. And Marie, unsuspicious, put her arms about the shoulders of the Pharisee and helped him to rise. They ate their supper with a narrow table between them. If there had been a doubt in Blake's mind before that, the half hour in which she sat facing him dispelled it utterly. At first the amazing beauty of Thoreau's wife had impinged itself upon his senses with something of a shock. But he was cool now. He was again master of his old cunning. Pitilessly and without conscience, he was marshaling the crafty forces of his brute nature for this new and more thrilling fight - the fight for a woman.

That in representing the Law he was pledged to virtue as well as order had never entered into his code of life. To him the Law was force - power. It had exalted him. It had forged an iron mask over the face of his savagery. And it was the savage that was dominant in him now. He saw in Marie's dark eyes a great love - love for a murderer.

It was not his thought that he might alienate that. For that look, turned upon himself, he would have sacrificed his whole world as it had previously existed. He was scheming beyond that impossibility, measuring her even as he called himself Duval, counting - not his chances of success, but the length of time it would take him to succeed.

He had never failed. A man had never beaten him. A woman had never tricked him. And he granted no possibility of failure now. But - HOW? That was the question that writhed and twisted itself in his brain even as he smiled at her over the table and told her of the black days of Jan's sickness up on the edge of the Barren.

And then it came to him - all at once. Marie did not see. She did not FEEL. She had no suspicion of this loyal friend of her husband's.

Blake's heart pounded triumphant. He hobbled back to the cot, leaning on Marie slim shoulder; and as he hobbled he told her how he had helped Jan into his cabin in just this same way, and how at the end Jan had collapsed - just as he collapsed when he came to the cot. He pulled Marie down with him - accidentally. His lips touched her head. He laughed.

For a few moments he was like a drunken man in his new joy. Willingly he would have gambled his life on his chance of winning. But confidence displaced none of his cunning. He rubbed his hands and said:

"Gawd, but won't it be a surprise for Jan? I told him that some day I'd come. I told him!"

It would be a tremendous joke - this surprise he had in store for Jan. He chuckled over it again and again as Marie went about her work; and Marie's face flushed and her eyes were bright and she laughed softly at this great love which Duval betrayed for her husband. No; even the loss of his dogs and his outfit couldn't spoil his pleasure! Why should it? He could get other dogs and another outfit - but it had been three years since he had seen Jan Thoreau! When Marie had finished her work he put his hand suddenly to his eyes and said:

"Peste! but last night's storm must have hurt my eyes. The light blinds them, ma cheri. Will you put it out, and sit down near me, so that I can see you as you talk, and tell me all that has happened to Jan Thoreau since that winter three years ago?"

She put out the light, and threw open the door of the box-stove. In the dim firelight she sat on a stool beside Blake's cot. Her faith in him was like that of a child. She was twenty-two. Blake was fifteen years older. She felt the immense superiority of his age.

This man, you must understand, had been more than a brother to Jan. He had been a father. He had risked his life. He had saved him from death. And Marie, as she sat at his side, did not think of him as a young man - thirty-seven. She talked to him as she might have talked to an elder brother of Jan's, and with something like the same reverence in her voice.

It was unfortunate - for her - that Jan had loved Duval, and that he had never tired of telling her about him. And now, when Blake's caution warned him to lie no more about the days of plague in Duval's cabin, she told him - as he had asked her - about herself and Jan; how they had lived during the last three years, the important things that had happened to them, and what they were looking forward to. He caught the low note of happiness that ran through her voice; and with a laugh, a laugh that sounded real and wholesome, he put out his hand in the darkness - for the fire had burned itself low - and stroked her hair. She did not shrink from the caress. He was happy because THEY were happy. That was her thought! And Blake did not go too far.

She went on, telling Jan's life away, betraying him In her happiness, crucifying him in her faith. Blake knew that she was telling the truth. She did not know that Jan had killed Francois Breault, and she believed that he would surely return - in three days. And the way he had left her that morning! Yes, she confided even that to this big brother of Jan, her cheeks flushing hotly in the darkness - how he had hated to go, and held her a long time in his arms before he tore himself away.

Had he taken his fiddle along with him? Yes - always that. Next to herself he loved his violin. Oo-oo - no, no - she was not jealous of the violin! Blake laughed - such a big, healthy, happy laugh, with an odd tremble in it. He stroked her hair again, and his fingers lay for an instant against her warm cheek.

And then, quite casually, he played his second big card.

"A man was found dead on the trail yesterday," he said. "Some one killed him. He had a bullet through his lung. He was the mail-runner, Francois Breault."

It was then, when he said that Breault had been murdered, that Blake's hand touched Marie's cheek and fell to her shoulder. It was too dark in the cabin to see. But under his hand he felt her grow suddenly rigid, and for a moment or two she seemed to stop breathing. In the gloom Blake's lips were smiling. He had struck, and he needed no light to see the effect.

"Francois - Breault!" he heard her breathe at last, as if she was fighting to keep something from choking her. "Francois Breault - dead - killed by someone - "

She rose slowly. His eyes followed her, a shadow in the gloom as she moved toward the stove. He heard her strike a match, and when she turned toward him again in the light of the oil-lamp, her face was pale and her eyes were big and staring. He swung himself to the edge of the cot, his pulse beating with the savage thrill of the inquisitor. Yet he knew that it was not quite time for him to disclose himself - not quite. He did not dread the moment when he would rise and tell her that he was not injured, and that he was not M'sieu Duval, but Corporal Blake of the Royal Mounted Police. He was eager for that moment. But he waited - discreetly. When the trap was sprung there would be no escape.

"You are sure - it was Francois Breault?" she said at last.

He nodded.

"Yes, the mail-runner. You knew him?"

She had moved to the table, and her hand was gripping the edge of it. For a space she did not answer him, but seemed to be looking somewhere through the cabin walls - a long way off. Ferret-like, he was watching her, and saw his opportunity. How splendidly fate was playing his way!

He rose to his feet and hobbled painfully to her, a splendid hypocrite, a magnificent dissembler. He seized her hand and held it in both his own. It was small and soft, but strangely cold.

"Ma cheri - my dear child - what makes you look like that? What has the death of Francois Breault to do with you - you and Jan?"

It was the voice of a friend, a brother, low, sympathetic, filled just enough with anxiety. Only last winter, in just that way, it had won the confidence and roused the hope of Pierrot's wife, over on the Athabasca. In the summer that followed they hanged Pierrot. Gently Blake spoke the words again. Marie's lips trembled. Her great eyes were looking at him - straight into his soul, it seemed.

"You may tell me, ma cheri," he encouraged, barely above a whisper. "I am Duval. And Jan - I love Jan."

He drew her back toward the cot, dragging his limb painfully, and seated her again upon the stool. He sat beside her, still holding her hand, patting it, encouraging her. The color was coming back into Marie's cheeks. Her lips were growing full and red again, and suddenly she gave a trembling little laugh as she looked up into Blake's face. His presence began to dispel the terror that had possessed her all at once.

"Tell me, Marie."

He saw the shudder that passed through her slim shoulders.

"They had a fight - here - in this cabin - three days ago," she confessed. "It must have been - the day - he was killed."

Blake knew the wild thought that was in her heart as she watched him. The muscles of his jaws tightened. His shoulders grew tense. He looked over her head as if he, too, saw something beyond the cabin walls. It was Marie's hand that gripped his now, and her voice, panting almost, was filled with an agonized protest.

"No, no, no - it was not Jan," she moaned. "It was not Jan who killed him!"

"Hush!" said Blake.

He looked about him as if there was a chance that someone might hear the fatal words she had spoken. It was a splendid bit of acting, almost unconscious, and tremendously effective. The expression in his face stabbed to her heart like a cold knife. Convulsively her fingers clutched more tightly at his hands. He might as well have spoken the words: "It was Jan, then, who killed Francois Breault!"

Instead of that he said:

"You must tell me everything, Marie. How did it happen? Why did they fight? And why has Jan gone away so soon after the killing? For Jan's sake, you must tell me - everything."

He waited. It seemed to him that he could hear the fighting struggle in Marie's breast. Then she began, brokenly, a little at a time, now and then barely whispering the story. It was a woman's story, and she told it like a woman, from the beginning. Perhaps at one time the rivalry between Jan Thoreau and Francois Breault, and their struggle for her love, had made her heart beat faster and her cheeks flush warm with a woman's pride of conquest, even though she had loved one and had hated the other. None of that pride was in her voice now, except when she spoke of Jan.

"Yes - like that - children together - we grew up," she confided. "It was down there at Wollaston Post, in the heart of the big forests, and when I was a baby it was

Jan who carried me about on his shoulders. Oui, even then he played the violin. I loved it. I loved Jan - always. Later, when I was seventeen, Francois Breault came."

She was trembling.

"Jan has told me a little about those days," lied Blake. "Tell me the rest, Marie."

"I - I knew I was going to be Jan's wife," she went on, the hands she had withdrawn from his twisting nervously in her lap. "We both knew. And yet - he had not spoken - he had not been definite. Oo-oo, do you understand, M'sieu Duval? It was my fault at the beginning! Francois Breault loved me. And so - I played with him - only a little, m'sieu! - to frighten Jan into the thought that he might lose me. I did not know what I was doing. No - no; I didn't understand.

"Jan and I were married, and on the day Jan saw the missioner - a week before we were made man and wife - Francois Beault came in from the trail to see me, and I confessed to him, and asked his forgiveness. We were alone. And he - Francois Breault - was like a madman."

She was panting. Her hands were clenched. "If Jan hadn't heard my cries, and come just in time - " she breathed.

Her blazing eyes looked up into Blake's face. He understood, and nodded.

"And it was like that - again - three days ago," she continued. "I hadn't seen Breault in two years - two years ago down at Wollaston Post. And he was mad. Yes, he must have been mad when he came three days ago. I don't know that he came so much for me as it was to kill Jan, He said it was Jan. Ugh, and it was here - in the cabin - that they fought!"

"And Jan - punished him," said Blake in a low voice.

Again the convulsive shudder swept through Marie's shoulders.

"It was strange - what happened, m'sieu. I was going to shoot. Yes, I would have shot him when the chance came. But all at once Francois Breault sprang back to the door, and he cried: 'Jan Thoreau, I am mad - mad! Great God, what have I done?' Yes, he said that, m'sieu, those very words - and then he was gone."

"And that same day - a little later - Jan went away from the cabin, and was gone a long time," whispered Blake. "Was it not so, Marie?"

"Yes; he went to his trap-line, m'sieu."

For the first time Blake made a movement. He took her face boldly between his two hands, and turned it so that her staring eyes were looking straight into his own. Every fiber in his body was trembling with the thrill of his monstrous triumph. "My dear little girl, I must tell you the truth," he said. "Your husband, Jan, did not go to his trap-line three days ago. He followed Francois Breault, and killed him. And I am not John Duval. I am Corporal Blake of the Mounted Police, and I have come to get Jan, that he may be hanged by the neck until he is dead for his crime. I came for that. But I have changed my mind. I have seen you, and for you I would give even a murderer his life. Do you understand? For YOU - YOU - YOU - "

And then came the grand finale, just as he had planned it. His words had stupefied her. She made no movement, no sound - only her great eyes seemed alive. And suddenly he swept her into his arms with the wild passion of a beast. How long she lay against his breast, his arms crushing her, his hot lips on her face, she did not know.

The world had grown suddenly dark. But in that darkness she heard his voice; and what it was saying roused her at last from the deadliness of her stupor. She strained against him, and with a wild cry broke from his arms, and staggered across the cabin floor to the door of her bedroom. Blake did not pursue her. He let the darkness of that room shut her in. He had told her - and she understood.

He shrugged his shoulders as he rose to his feet. Quite calmly, in spite of the wild rush of blood through his body, he went to the cabin door, opened it, and looked out into the night. It was full of stars, and quiet.

It was quiet in that inner room, too - so quiet that one might fancy he could hear the beating of a heart. Marie had flung herself in the farthest corner, beyond the bed. And there her hand had touched something. It was cold - the chill of steel. She could almost have screamed, in the mighty reaction that swept through her like an electric shock. But her lips were dumb and her hand clutched tighter at the cold thing.

She drew it toward her inch by inch, and leveled it across the bed. It was Jan's goose-gun, loaded with buck-shot. There was a single metallic click as she drew the hammer back. In the doorway, looking at the stars, Blake did not hear.

Marie waited. She was not reasoning things now, except that in the outer room there was a serpent that she must kill. She would kill him as he came between her and the light; then she would follow over Jan's trail, overtake him somewhere, and they would flee together. Of that much she thought ahead. But chiefly her mind, her eyes, her brain, her whole being, were concentrated on the twelve-inch opening between the bedroom door and the outer room. The serpent would soon appear there. And then -

She heard the cabin door close, and Blake's footsteps approaching. Her body did not tremble now. Her forefinger was steady on the trigger. She held her breath - and waited. Blake came to the deadline and stopped. She could see one arm and a part of his shoulder. But that was not enough. Another half step - six inches - four even, and she would fire. Her heart pounded like a tiny hammer in her breast.

And then the very life in her body seemed to stand still. The cabin door had opened suddenly, and someone had entered. In that moment she would have fired, for she knew that it must be Jan who had returned. But Blake had moved. And now, with her finger on the trigger, she heard his cry of amazement:

"Sergeant Fitzgerald!"

"Yes. Put up your gun, Corporal. Have you got Jan Thoreau?"

"He - is gone."

"That is lucky for us." It was the stranger's voice, filled with a great relief. "I have traveled fast to overtake you. Matao, the half-breed, was stabbed in a quarrel soon after you left; and before he died he confessed to killing Breault. The evidence is conclusive. Ugh, but this fire is good! Anybody at home?"

"Yes," said Blake slowly. "Mrs. Thoreau - is - at home."

L'ANGE

She stood in the doorway of a log cabin that was overgrown with woodvine and mellow with the dull red glow of the climbing bakneesh, with the warmth of the late summer sun falling upon her bare head. Cummins' shout had brought her to the door when we were still half a rifle shot down the river; a second shout, close to shore, brought her running down toward me. In that first view that I had of her, I called her beautiful. It was chiefly, I believe, because of her splendid hair. John Cummins' shout of homecoming had caught her with it undone, and she greeted us with the dark and lustrous masses of it sweeping about her shoulders and down to her hips. That is, she greeted Cummins, for he had been gone for nearly a month. I busied myself with the canoe for that first half minute or so.

Then it was that I received my introduction and for the first time touched the hand of Melisse Cummins, the Florence Nightingale of several thousand square miles of northern wilderness. I saw, then, that what I had at first taken for our own hothouse variety of beauty was a different thing entirely, a type that would have disappointed many because of its strength and firmness. Her hair was a glory, brown and soft. No woman could have criticized its loveliness. But the flush that I had seen in her face, flower-like at a short distance, was a tan that was almost a man's tan. Her eyes were of a deep blue and as clear as the sky; but in them, too, there was a strength that was not altogether feminine. There was strength in her face, strength in the poise of her firm neck, strength in every movement of her limbs and body. When she spoke, it was in a voice which, like her hair, was adorable. I had never heard a sweeter voice , and her firm mouth was all at once not only gentle and womanly, but almost girlishly pretty.

I could understand, now, why Melisse Cummins was the heroine of a hundred true tales of the wilderness, and I could understand as well why there was scarcely a cabin or an Indian hut in that ten thousand square miles of wilderness in which she had not, at one time or another, been spoken of as "L'ange Meleese." And yet, unlike that other "angel" of flesh and blood, Florence Nightingale, the story of Melisse Cummins and her work will live and die with her in that little cabin two hundred miles straight north of civilization. No, that is wrong. For the wilderness will remember. It will remember, as it has remembered Father Duchene and the Missioner of Lac Bain and the heroic days of the early voyageurs. A hundred "Meleeses" will bear her memory in name - for all who speak her name call her "Meleese," and not Melisse.

The wilderness itself may never forget, as it has never forgotten beautiful Jeanne D'Arcambal, who lived and died on the shore of the great bay more than one hundred and sixty years ago. It will never forget the great heart this woman has given to her "people" from the days of girlhood; it will not forget the thousand perils she faced to seek out the sick, the plague-stricken and the starving; in old age there will still be those who will remember the first prayers to the real God that she taught them in childhood; and children still to come, in cabin, tepee and hut, will live to bless the memory of L'ange Meleese, who made possible for them a new birthright and who in the wild places lived to the full measure and glory of the Golden Rule.

To find Meleese Cummins and her home in the wilderness, one must start at Le Pas as the last outpost of civilization and strike northward through the long Pelican Lake waterways to Reindeer Lake. Nearly forty miles up the east shore of the lake, the adventurer will come to the mouth of the Gray Loon - narrow and silent stream that winds under overhanging forests - and after that a two-hours' journey in a canoe will bring one to the Cummins' cabin.

It is set in a clearing, with the thick spruce and balsam and cedar hemming it in, and a tall ridge capped with golden birch rising behind it. In that clearing John Cummins raises a little fruit and a few vegetables during the summer months; but it is chiefly given up to three or four huge plots of scarlet moose-flowers, a garden of Labrador tea, and wild flowering plants and vines of half a dozen varieties. And where the radiant moose-flowers grow thickest, screened from the view of the cabin by a few cedars and balsams, are the rough wooden slabs that mark seven graves. Six of them are the graves of children - little ones who died deep in the wilderness and whose tiny bodies Meleese Cummins could not leave to the savage and pitiless loneliness of the forests, but whom she has brought together that they might have company in what she calls her, "Little Garden of God."

Those little graves tell the story of Meleese - the

woman who, all heart and soul, has buried her own one little babe in that garden of flowers. One of the slabs marks the grave of an Indian baby, whose little dead body Meleese Cummins carried to her cabin in her own strong arms from twenty miles back in the forest, when the temperature was fifty degrees below zero. Another of them, a baby boy, a French half-breed and his wife brought down from fifty miles up the Reindeer and begged "L'ange Meleese" to let it rest with the others, where "it might not be lonely and would not be frightened by the howl of the wolves." It was a wild and half Indian mother who said that!

It was almost twenty years ago that the romance began in the lives of John and Meleese Cummins. Meleese was then ten years old; and she still remembers as vividly as though they were but memories of yesterday the fears and wild tales of that one terrible winter when the "Red Terror" - the smallpox - swept in a pitiless plague of death throughout the northern wilderness. It was then that there came down from the north, one bitter cold day, a ragged and half-starved boy, whose mother and father had died of the plague in a little cabin fifty miles away, and who from the day he staggered into the home of Henry Janesse, became Meleese's playmate and chum. This boy was John Cummins.

When Janesse moved to Fort Churchill, where Meleese might learn more in the way of reading and writing and books than her parents could teach her, John Cummins went with her. He went with them to Nelson House, and from there to Split Lake, where Janesse died. From that time, at the age of eighteen, he became the head and support of the home. When he was twenty and Meleese eighteen, the two were married by a missioner from Nelson House. The following autumn the young wife's mother died, and that winter Meleese began her remarkable work among her "people."

In their little cabin on the Gray Loon, one will hear John Cummins say but little about himself; but there is a glow in his eyes and a flush in his cheeks as he tells of that first day he came home from a three-days journey over a long trap line to find his home cold and fireless, and a note written by Meleese telling him that she had gone with a twelve-year-old boy who had brought her word through twenty miles of forest that his mother was dying. That first "case" was more terrible for John Cummins than for his wife, for it turned out to be smallpox, and for six weeks Meleese would allow him to come no nearer than the edge of the clearing' in which the pest-ridden cabin stood. First the mother, and then the boy, she nursed back to life, locking the door against the two husbands, who built themselves a shack in the edge of the forest. Half a dozen times Meleese Cummins has gone through ordeals like that unscathed. Once it was to nurse a young Indian mother through the dread disease, and again she went into a French trapper's cabin where husband, wife and daughter were all sick with the malady. At these times, when the "call" came to Meleese from a far cabin or tepee, John Cummins would give up the duties of his trap line to accompany her, and would pitch his tent or make him a shack close by, where he could watch over her, hunt food for the afflicted people and keep up the stack of needed firewood and water.

But there were times when the "calls" came during the husband's absence, and, if they were urgent, Meleese went alone, trusting to her own splendid strength and courage. A half-breed woman came to her one day, in the dead of winter, from twenty miles across the lake. Her husband had frozen one of his feet, and the "frost malady" would kill him, she said, unless he had help. Scarcely knowing what she could do in such a case, Meleese left a note for her husband, and on snowshoes the two heroic women set off across the wind-swept and unsheltered lake, with the thermometer fifty degrees below zero. It was a terrible venture, but the two won out. When Meleese saw the frozen man, she knew that there was but one thing to do, and with all the courage of her splendid heart she amputated his foot. The torture of that terrible hour no one will ever know. But when John Cummins returned to his home and, wild with fear, followed across the lake, he scarcely recognized the Meleese who flung herself sobbing into his arms when he found her. For two weeks after that Meleese herself was sick. Thus, through the course of years, it came about that it was, indeed, a stranger in the land who had not heard her name. During the summer months Meleese's work, in place of duty, was a pleasure. With her husband she made canoe journeys for fifty miles about her home, hearing with her the teachings of cleanliness, of health and of God. She was the first to hold to her own loving breast many little children who came into their wild and desolate inheritance of life. She was the first to teach a hundred childish lips to say "Now I lay me down to sleep," and more than one woman she made to see the clear and starry way to brighter life.

Far up on Reindeer Lake, close to the shore, there is a towering "lob-stick tree" - which is a tall spruce or cedar lopped of all its branches to the very crest, which is trimmed in the form of a plume. A tree thus shriven and trimmed is the Cree cenotaph to one held in almost spiritual reverence, and the tree far up on Reindeer Lake is one of the half dozen or more "lob-sticks" dedicated to Meleese. Six weeks Meleese and John Cummins spent in an Indian camp at this point, and when at last the two bade their primitive friends good-bye and left for home, the little Indian children and the women followed their canoe along the edge of a stream and flung handfuls of flowers after them.

Of what Meleese Cummins and her husband know of the great outside world, or of what they do not know, it is wisest to leave unsaid. Details have often marred a picture. They are children of the wilderness, born of that wilderness, bred of it, and life of it - a beating and palpitating part of a world which few can understand. I doubt if one or the other has ever heard of a William Shakespeare or a Tennyson, for it has not been in my mind or desire to ask; but they do know the human heart as it beats and throbs in a land that is desolation and loneliness, where poetry runs not in lines and meters, but in the bloom of the wild flower, the rush of the rapid, the thunder of the waterfall and the murmuring of the wind in the spruce tops; where drama exists not in the epic lines of literature, but in the hunt cry of the wolf, the death dirges of the storms that wail down from the Barrens, and in the strange cries that rise up out of the silent forests, where for a half of each year life is that endless strife that leaves behind only those whom we term the survival of the fittest.

THE CASE OF BEAUVAIS

Madness? Perhaps. And yet if it was madness. . . .

But strange things happen up there, gentlemen. I have found it sometimes hard to define that word. There are so many kinds of madness, so many ways in which the human brain may go wrong; and so often it happens that what we call madness is both reasonable and just. It is so. Yes. A little reason is good for us, a little more makes wise men of some of us - but when our reason over-grows us and we reach too far, something breaks and we go insane.

But I will tell you the story. That is what you want to hear, and you expect that it will be prejudiced - that I will either deliberately attempt to protect and prolong a human life, or shorten and destroy it. I shall do neither, gentlemen of the Royal Mounted Police. I have a faith in you that is in its way an unbounded as my faith in God. I have looked up to you in all my life in the wilderness as the heart of chivalry and the soul of honor and fairness to all men. Pathfinders, men of iron, guardians of people and spaces of which civilization knows but little, I have taught my children of the forests to honor, obey and to trust you. And so I shall tell you the story without prejudice, with the gratitude of a missioner who has lived his life for forty years in the wilderness, gentlemen.

I am a Catholic. It is four hundred miles straight north by dog-sledge or snowshoe to my cabin, and this is the first time in nineteen years that I have been down to the edge of the big world which I remember now as little more than a dream. But up there I knew that my duty lay, just at the edge of the Big Barren. See! My hands are knotted like the snarl of a tree. The glare of your lights hurts my eyes. I traveled to-day in the middle of your street because my moccasined feet stumbled on the smoothness of your walks. People stared, and some of them laughed.

Forty years I have lived in another world. You - and especially you gentlemen who have trailed in the Patrols of the north - know what that world is. As it shapes different hands, as it trains different feet, as it gives to us different eyes, so also it has bred into my forest children hearts and souls that may be a little different, and a code of right and wrong that too frequently has had no court of law to guide it. So judge fairly, gentlemen of the Royal Mounted Police! Understand, if you can.

It was a terrible winter - that winter of Le Mort Rouge. So far down as men and children now living will remember, it will be called by my people the winter of Famine and Red Death. Starvation, gentlemen - and the smallpox. People died like - what shall I say? It is not easy to describe a thing like that. They died in tepees. They died in shacks. They died on the trail. From late December until March I said my prayers over the dead. You are wondering what all this has to do with my story; why it matters that the caribou had migrated in vast herds to the westward, and there was no food; why it matters that there were famine and plague in the great unknown land, and that people were dying and our world going through a cataclysm. My backwoods eyes can see your thought. What has all this to do with Joseph Brecht? What has it to do with Andre Beauvais? Why does this little forest priest take up so much time in telling so little? you ask. And because it has its place - because it has its meaning - I ask you for permission to tell my story in my own way. For these sufferings, this hunger and pestilence and death, had a strange and terrible effect on many human creatures that were left alive when spring came. It was like a great storm that had swept through a forest of tall trees. A storm of suffering that left heads bowed, shoulders bent, and minds gone. Yes, GONE!

Since that winter of Le Mort Rouge I know of eyes into which the life of laughter will never come again; I know of strong men who became as little children; I have seen faces that were fair with youth shrivel into age - and my people call it noot' akutawin keskwawin - the cold and hungry madness. May God help Andre Beauvais!

I will tell the story now.

It was in June. The last of the mush-snows had gone early, nearly a fortnight before, and the waters were free from ice, when word was brought to me that Father Boget was dying at Old Fort Reliance. Father Boget was twenty years older than I, and I called him mon pere. He was a father to me in our earlier years. I made haste to reach him that I might hold his hand before he died, if that was possible. And you, Sergeant McVeigh, who have spent years in that country of the Great Slave, know what a race with death from Christie Bay to Old Fort Eeliance would be. To follow the broken and twisted waters of the Great Slave would mean two hundred miles, while to cut straight across the land by smaller streams and lakelets meant less than seventy. But on your maps that space of seventy miles is a blank. You have in it no streams and no larger waters. You know little of it. But I can tell you, for I have been though it. It is a Lost Hell. It is a vast country in which berry bushes grow abundantly, but on which there are no berries, where there are forests and swamps, but not a living creature to inhabit them; a country of water in which there are no fish, of air in which there are no birds, of plants without flowers - a reeking, stinking country of brimstone, a hell. In your Blue Books you have called it the Sulphur Country. And this country, as you draw a line from Christie Bay to Old Fort Reliance, is straight between. Mon pere was dying, and my time was short. I decided to venture it - cut across that Sulphur Country, and I sought for a man to accompany me. I could find none. To the Indian it was the land of Wetikoo - the Devil Country; to the Breeds it was filled with horror. Forty miles distant there was a man I knew would go, a white man. But to reach him would lose me three days, and I was about to set out alone when the stranger came. He was, indeed, a strange man. When he came to what I called my chateau, from nowhere, going nowhere, I hardly knew whether to call him young or old. But I made my guess. That terrib le winter had branded him. When I asked him his name, he said:

"I am a wanderer, and in wandering I have lost my name. Call me M'sieu."

I found this was a long speech for him, that his tongue was tied by a horrible silence. When I told him where I was going, and described the country I was going through, and that I wanted a man, he merely nodded that he would accompany me.

We started in a canoe, and I placed him ahead of me so that I could make out, if I could, something of what he was. His hair was dark. His beard was dark. His eyes were sunken but strangely clear. They puzzled me. They were always questing. Always seeking. And always expecting, it seemed to me. A man of unfathomable mystery, of unutterable tragedy, of a silence that was almost inhuman. Was he mad? I ask you, gentlemen - was he mad? And I leave the answer to you. To me he was good. When I told him what mon pere had been to me, and that I wanted to reach him before he died, he spoke no word of hope or sympathy - but worked until his muscles cracked. We ate together, we drank together, we slept side by side - and it was like eating and drinking and sleeping with a sphinx which some strange miracle had endowed with life.

The second day we entered the Sulphur Country. The stink of it was in our nostrils that second night we camped. The moon rose, and we saw it as if through the fumes of a yellow smoke. Far behind us we heard a wolf howl, and it was the last sound of life. With the dawn we went on. We passed through broad, low morasses out of which rose the sulphurous fogs. In many places the water we touched with our hands was hot; in other places the forests we paddled through were so dense they were almost tropical. And lifeless. Still, with the stillness of death for thousands and perhaps tens of thousands of years. The food we ate seemed saturated with the vileness of sulphur; it seeped into our water-bags; it turned us to the color of saffron; it was terrible, frightening, inconceivable. And still we went on by compass, and M'sieu showed no fear - even less, gentlemen, than did I.

And then, on the third day - in the heart of this diseased and horrible region - we made a discovery that drew a strange cry even from those mysteriously silent lips of M'sieu.

It was the print of a naked human foot in a bar of mud.

How it came there, why it was there, and why if was a naked foot I suppose were the first thoughts that leaped into our startled minds. What man could live in these infernal regions? WAS it a man, or was it the footprint of some primeval ape, a monstrous survival of the centuries?

The trail led through a steaming slough in which the mud and water were tepid and which grew rank with yellow reeds and thick grasses - grasses that were almost flesh-like, it seemed to me, as if swollen and about to burst from some dreadful disease, Perhaps your scientists can tell why sulphur has this effect on vegetation. It is so; there was sulphur in the very wood we burned. Through those reeds and grasses we soon found where a narrow trail was beaten, and then we came to a rise of land sheltered in timber, a sort of hill in that flat world, and on the crest of this hill we found a cabin.

Yes, a cabin; a cabin built roughly of logs, and it was yellow with sulphur, as if painted. We went inside and we found there the man whom you know as Joseph Brecht. I did not look at M'sieu when he first rose before us, but I heard a great gasp from his throat behind me. And I think I stood as if life had suddenly gone out of me. Joseph Brecht was half naked. His feet were bare. He looked like a wild man, with his uncut hair - a wild man except that his face was smooth. Curious that a man would shave there! And not so odd, perhaps, when one knows how a beard gathers sulphur. He had risen from a cot on which there was a bed of boughs, and in the light that came in through the open door he looked terribly emaciated, with the skin drawn tightly over his cheek bones. It was he who spoke first.

"I am glad you have come," he said, his eyes staring wildly. "I guess I am dying. Some water, please. There is a spring back of the cabin."

Quite sanely he spoke, and yet the words were scarcely out of his mouth when he fell back upon the cot, his eyes rolling in the top of his head, his mouth agape, his breath coming in great panting gasps. It was a strange sickness. I will not trouble you with all the details. You are anxious for the story - the tragedy - which alone will count with you gentlemen of the law. It came out in his fever, and in the fits of sanity into which he at times succeeded in rousing himself. His name, he said, was Joseph Brecht. For two years he had lived in that sulphur hell. He had, by accident, found the spring of fresh, sweet water trickling out of the hill - another miracle for which I have not tried to account; he built his cabin; for two years he had gone with his canoe to the shore of the great Slave, forty miles distant, for the food he ate. But WHY was he here? That was the story that came bit by bit, half in his fever, half in his sanity. I will tell it in my own words. He was a Government man, mapping out the last timber lines along the edge of the Great Barren, when he first met Andre Beauvais and his wife, Marie. An accident took him to their cabin, a sprained leg. Andre was a fox-hunter, and it was when he was coming home from one of his trips that he found Joseph Brecht helpless in the deep snow, and carried him on his shoulders to his cabin.

Ah, gentlemen, it was the old story - the story old as time. In his sanity he told us about Marie, I hovering over him closely, M'sieu sitting back in the shadows. She was like some wonderful wildflower, French, a little Indian. He told us how her long black hair would stream in a shining cascade, soft as the breast of a swan, to her knees and below; how it would hang again in two great, lustrous braids, and how her eyes were limpid pools that set his soul afire, and how her slim, beautiful body filled him with a monstrous desire. She must have been beautiful. And her husband, Andre Beauvais, worshipped her, and the ground she trod on. And he had the faith in her that a mother has in her child. It was a sublime love, and Joseph Brecht told us about it as he lay there, dying, as he supposed. In that faith of his Andre went unsuspectingly to his trap-lines and his poison-trails, and Marie and Joseph were for many hours at a time alone, sometimes for a day, sometimes for two days, and occasionally for three, for even after his limb had regained its strength Joseph feigned that it was bad. It was a hard fight, he said - a hard fight for him to win her; but win her he did, utterly, absolutely, heart, body and soul. Remember, he was from the South, with all its power of language, all its tricks of love, all its furtiveness of argument, a strong man with a strong mind - and she had lived all her life in the wilderness. She was no match for him. She surrendered. He told us how, after that, he would unbind her wonderful hair and pillow his face in it; how he lived in a heaven of transport, how utterly she gave herself to him in those times when Andre, was away.

Did he love her?

Yes, in that mad passion of the brute. But not as you and I might love a woman, gentlemen. Not as Andre loved her. Whether she had a heart or a soul it did not matter. His eyes were blind with an insensate joy when he shrouded himself in her wonderful hair. To see the wild color painting her face like a flower filled his veins with fire. The beauty of her, the touch of her, the mad beat of her heart against him made him like a drunken man in his triumph. Love? Yes, the love of the brute! He prolonged his stay. He had no idea of taking her with him. When the time came, he would go. Day after day, week after week he put it off, feigning that the bone of his leg was affected, and Andre Beauvais treated him like a brother. He told us all this as he lay there in his cabin in that sulphur hell. I am a man of God, and I do not lie.

Is there need to tell you that Andre discovered them? Yes, he found them - and with that wonderful hair of hers so closely about them that he was still bound in the tresses when the discovery came.

Andre had come in exhausted, and unexpectedly. There was a terrible fight, and in spite of his exhaustion he would have killed Joseph Brecht if at the last moment the latter had not drawn his revolver. After all is said and done, gentlemen, can a woman love but once? Joseph Brecht fired. In that infinitesimal moment between the leveling of the gun and the firing of the shot Marie Beauvais found answer to that question. Who was it she loved? She sprang to her husband's breast, sheltering him with the body that had been disloyal to its soul, and she died there - with a bullet through her heart.

Joseph Brecht told us how, in the horror of his work - and possessed now by a terrible fear - he ran from the cabin and fled for his life. And Andre Beauvais must have remained with his dead. For it was many hours later before he took up the trail of the man whom he made solemn oath to his God to kill. Like a hunted hare, Joseph Brecht eluded him, and it was weeks before the fox-trapper came upon him. Andre Beauvais scorned to kill him from ambush. He wanted to choke his life out slowly, with his two hands, and he attacked him openly and fairly.

And in that cabin - gasping for breath, dying as he thought, Joseph Brecht said to us: "It was one or the other. He had the best of me. I drew my revolver again - and killed him, killed Andre Beauvais, as I had killed his wife, Marie!"

Here in the South Joseph Brecht might not have been a bad man, gentlemen. In every man's heart there is a devil, but we do not know the man as bad until the devil is roused. And passion, the mad passion for a woman, had roused him. Now that it had made twice a murderer of him the devil slunk back into his hiding, and the man who had once been the clean-living, red-blooded Joseph Brecht was only a husk without a heart, slinking from place to place in the evasion of justice. For you men of the Royal Mounted Police were on his trail. You would have caught him, but you did not think of seeking for him in the Sulphur Hell. For two years he had lived there, and when he finished his story he was sitting on the edge of the cot, quite sane, gentlemen.

And for the first time M'sieu, my comrade, spoke.

"Let us bring up the dunnage from the canoe, mon pere."

He led the way out of the cabin, and I followed. We were fifty steps away when he stopped suddenly.

"Ah," he said, "I have forgotten something. I will overtake you."

He turned back to the cabin, and I went on to the canoe.

He did not join me. When I returned with my burden, M'sieu appeared at the door. He amazed me, startled me, I will say, gentlemen. I could not imagine such a change as I saw in him - that man of horrible silence, of grim, dark mystery. He was smiling; his white teeth shone; his voice was the voice of another man. He seemed to me ten years younger as he stood there, and as I dropped my load and went in he was laughing, and his hand was laid pleasantly on my shoulder.

Across the cot, with his head stretched down to the floor, his eyes bulging and his jaws agape, lay Joseph Brecht. I sprang to him. He was dead. And then I SAW Gentlemen, he had been choked to death!

"He made one leetle meestake, mon pere. Andre Beauvais did not die. I am Andre Beauvais."

That is all, gentlemen of the Royal Mounted. May the Law have mercy!

THE OTHER MAN'S WIFE

Thornton wasn't the sort of man in whom you'd expect to find the devil lurking. He was big, blond, and broad-shouldered. When I first saw him I thought he was an Englishman. That was at the post at Lac la Biche, six hundred miles north of civilization. Scotty and I had been doing some exploration work for the government, and for more than six months we hadn't seen a real white man who looked like home.

We came in late at night, and the factor gave us a room in his house. When we looked out of our window in the morning, we saw a little shack about a hundred feet away, and in front of that shack was Thornton, only half dressed, stretching himself in the sun, and LAUGHING. There wasn't anything to laugh at, but we could see his teeth shining white, and he grinned every minute while he went through a sort of setting-up exercise.

When you begin to analyze a man, there is always some one human trait that rises above all others, and that laugh was Thornton's. Even the wolfish sledge-dogs at the post would wag their tails when they heard it.

We soon established friendly relations, but I could not get very far beyond the laugh. Indeed, Thornton was a mystery. DeBar, the factor, said that he had dropped into the post six months before, with a pack on his back and a rifle over his shoulder. He had no business, apparently. He was not a propectory and it was only now and then that he used his rifle, and then only to shoot at marks.

One thing puzzled DeBar more than all else. Thornton worked like three men about the post, cutting winter fire-wood, helping to catch and clean the tons of whitefish which were stored away for the dogs in the company's ice-houses, and doing other things without end. For this he refused all payment except his rations.

Scotty continued eastward to Churchill, and for seven weeks I bunked with Thornton in the shack. At the end of those seven weeks I knew little more about Thornton than at the beginning. I never had a closer or more congenial chum, and yet in his conversation he never got beyond the big woods, the mountains, and the tangled swamps. He was educated and a gentleman, and I knew that in spite of his brown face and arms, his hard muscles and splendid health, he was three-quarters tenderfoot. But he loved the wilderness.

"I never knew what life could hold for a man until I came up here," he said to me one day, his gray eyes dancing in the light of a glorious sunset.

"I'm ten years younger than I was two years ago."

"You've been two years in the north?"

"A year and ten months," he replied.

Something brought to my lips the words that I had

forced back a score of times.

"What brought you up here, Thornton?"

"Two things," he said quietly, "a woman - and a scoundrel."

He said no more, and I did not press the matter. There was a strange tremble in his voice, something that I took to be a note of sadness; but when he turned from the sunset to me his eyes were filled with a yet stranger joy, and his big boyish laugh rang out with such wholesome infectiousness that I laughed with him, in spite of myself.

That night, in our shack, he produced a tightly bound bundle of letters about six inches thick, scattered them out before him on the table, and began reading them at random, while I sat bolstered back in my bunk, smoking and watching him. He was a curious study. Every little while I'd hear him chuckling and rumbling, his teeth agleam, and between these times he'd grow serious. Once I saw tears rolling down his cheeks.

He puzzled me; and the more he puzzled me, the better I liked him. Every night for a week he spent an hour or two reading those letters over and over again. I had a dozen opportunities to see that they were a woman's letters: but he never offered a word of explanation.

With the approach of September, I made preparations to leave for the south, by way of Moose Factory and the Albany.

"Why not go the shorter way - by the Reindeer Lake water route to Prince Albert ? " asked Thornton. "If you'll do that, I'll go with you."

His proposition delighted me, and we began planning for our trip. From that hour there came a curious change in Thornton. It was as if he had come into contact with some mysterious dynamo that had charged him with a strange nervous energy. We were two days in getting our stuff ready, and the night between he did not go to bed at all, but sat up reading the letters, smoking, and then reading over again what he had read half a hundred times before.

I was pretty well hardened, but during the first week of our canoe trip he nearly had me bushed a dozen times. He insisted on getting away before dawn, laughing, singing, and talking, and urged on the pace until sunset. I don't believe that he slept two hours a night. Often, when I woke up, I'd see him walking back and forth in the moonlight, humming softly to himself. There was almost a touch of madness in it all; but I knew that Thornton was sane.

One night - our fourteenth down - I awoke a little after midnight, and as usual looked about for Thornton. It was glorious night. There was a full moon over us, and with the lake at our feet, and the spruce and balsam forest on each side of us, the whole scene struck me as one of the most beautiful I had ever looked upon.

When I came out of our tent, Thornton was not in sight. Away across the lake I heard a moose calling. Back of me an owl hooted softly, and from miles away I could hear faintly the howling of a wolf. The night sounds were broken by my own startled cry as I felt a hand fall , without warning, upon my shoulder. It was Thornton. I had never seen his face as it looked just then.

"Isn't it beautiful - glorious?" he cried softly.

"It's wonderful!" I said. "You won't see this down there, Thornton!"

"Nor hear those sounds," he replied, his hand tightening on my arm. "We're pretty close to God up here, aren't we? She'll like it - I'll bring her back!"

"She!" He looked at me, his teeth shining in that wonderful silent laugh. "I'm going to tell you about it," he said. "I can't keep it in any longer. Let's go down by the lake."

We walked down and seated ourselves on the edge of a big rock.

"I told you that I came up here because of a woman - and a man," continued Thornton. "Well, I did. The man and woman were husband and wife, and I - "

He interrupted himself with one of his chuckling laughs. There was something in it that made me shudder.

"No use to tell you that I loved her," he went on. "I worshipped her. She was my life. And I believe she loved me as much. I might have added that there was a third thing that drove me up here - what remained of the rag end of a man's honor."

"I begin to understand," I said, as he paused. "You came up here to get away from the woman. But this woman - her husband - "

For the first time since I had known him I saw a flash of anger leap into Thornton's face. He struck his hand against the rock.

"Her husband was a scoundrel, a brute, who came home from his club drunk, a cheap money-spender, a man who wasn't fit to wipe the mud from her little feet, much less call her wife! He ought to have been shot. I can see it, now; and - well, I might as well tell you. I'm going back to her!"

"You are?" I cried. "Has she got a divorce? Is her husband still living?"

"No, she hasn't got a divorce, and her husband is still living; but for all that, we've arranged it. Those were her letters I've been reading, and she'll be at Prince Albert waiting for me on the 15th - three days from now. We shall be a little late, and that's why I'm hustling so. I've kept away from her for two years, but I can't do it any longer - and she says that if I do she'll kill herself. So there you have it. She's the sweetest, most beautiful girl in the whole world - eyes the color of those blue flowers you have up here, brown hair, and - but you've got to see her when we reach Prince Albert. You won't blame me for doing all this, then!"

I had nothing to say. At my silence he turned toward me suddenly, with that happy smile of his, and said again:

"I tell you that you won't blame me when you see her. You'll envy me, and you'll call me a confounded fool for staying away so long. It has been terribly hard for both of us. I'll wager that she's no sleepier than I am to-night, just from knowing that I'm hurrying to her."

"You're pretty confident," I could not help sneering. "I don't believe I'd wager much on such a woman. To be frank with you, Thornton, I don't care to meet her, so I'll decline your invitation. I've a little wife of my own, as true as steel, and I'd rather keep out of an affair like this. You understand?"

"Perfectly," said Thornton, and there was not the slightest ill-humor in his voice. "You - you think I am a cur?"

"If you have stolen another man's wife - yes."

"And the woman?"

"If she is betraying her husband, she is no better than you."

Thornton rose and stretched his long arms above his head.

"Isn't the moon glorious?" he cried exultantly. "She has never seen a moon like that. She has never seen a world like this. Do you know what we're going to do? We'll come up here and build a cabin, and - and she'll know what a real man is at last! She deserves it. And we'll have you up to visit us - you and your wife - two months out of each year. But then" - he turned and laughed squarely into my face - "you probably won't want your wife to know her."

"Probably not," I said, not without embarrassment.

"I don't blame you," he exclaimed, and before I could draw back he had caught my hand and was shaking it hard in his own. "Let's be friends a little longer, old man," he went on. "I know you'll change your mind about the little girl and me when we reach Prince Albert."

I didn't go to sleep again that night; and the half-dozen days that followed were unpleasant enough - for me, at least. In spite of my own coolness toward him, there was absolutely no change in Thornton. Not once did he make any further allusion to what he had told me.

As we drew near to our journey's end, his enthusiasm and good spirits increased. He had the bow end of the canoe, and I had abundant opportunity of watching him. It was impossible not to like him, even after I knew his story.

We reached Prince Albert on a Sunday, after three days' travel in a buckboard. When we drove up in front of the hotel, there was just one person on the long veranda looking out over the Saskatchewan. It was a woman, reading a book.

As he saw her, I heard a great breath heave up inside Thornton's chest. The woman looked up, stared for a moment, and then dropped her book with a welcoming cry such as I had never heard before in my life. She sprang down the steps, and Thornton leaped from the wagon. They met there a dozen paces from me, Thornton catching her in his arms, and the woman clasping her arms about his neck.

I heard her sobbing, and I saw Thornton kissing her again and again, and then the woman pulled his blond head down close to her face. It was sickening, knowing what I did, and I began helping the driver to throw off our dunnage.

In about two minutes I heard Thornton calling me.

I didn't turn my head. Then Thornton came to me, and as he straightened me around by the shoulders I caught a glimpse of the woman. He was right - she was very beautiful.

"I told you that her husband was a scoundrel and a rake," he said gently. "Well, he was - and I was that scoundrel! I came up here for a chance of redeeming myself, and your big, glorious North has made a man of me. Will you come and meet my wife?"

THE STRENGTH OF MEN

There was the scent of battle in the air. The whole of Porcupine City knew that it was coming, and every man and woman in its two hundred population held their breath in anticipation of the struggle between two men for a fortune - and a girl. For in some mysterious manner rumor of the girl had got abroad, passing from lip to lip, until even the children knew that there was some other thing than gold that would play a part in the fight between Clarry O'Grady and Jan Larose. On the surface it was not scheduled to be a fight with fists or guns. But in Porcupine City there were a few who knew the "inner story" - the story of the girl, as well as the gold, and those among them who feared the law would have arbitrated in a different manner for the two men if it had been in their power. But law is law, and the code was the code. There was no alternative. It was an unusual situation, and yet apparently simple of solution. Eighty miles north, as the canoe was driven, young Jan Larose had one day staked out a rich "find" at the headwaters of Pelican Creek. The same day, but later, Clarry O'Grady had driven his stakes beside Jan's. It had been a race to the mining recorder's office, and they had come in neck and neck. Popular sentiment favored Larose, the slim, quiet, dark-eyed half Frenchman. But there was the law, which had no sentiment. The recorder had sent an agent north to investigate. If there were two sets of stakes there could be but one verdict. Both claims would be thrown out, and then -

All knew what would happen, or thought that they knew. It would be a magnificent race to see who could set out fresh stakes and return to the recorder's office ahead of the other. It would be a fight of brawn and brain, unless - and those few who knew the "inner story" spoke softly among themselves.

An ox in strength, gigantic in build, with a face that for days had worn a sneering smile of triumph, O'Grady was already picked as a ten-to-one winner. He was a magnificent canoeman, no man in Porcupine City could equal him for endurance, and for his bow paddle he had the best Indian in the whole Reindeer Lake country. He stalked up and down the one street of Porcupine City, treating to drinks, cracking rough jokes, and offering wagers, while Jan Larose and his long-armed Cree sat quietly in the shade of the recorder's office waiting for the final moment to come.

There were a few of those who knew the "inner story" who saw something besides resignation and despair in Jan's quiet aloofness, and in the disconsolate droop of his head. His face turned a shade whiter when O'Grady passed near, dropping insult and taunt, and looking sidewise at him in a way that only HE could understand. But he made no retort, though his dark eyes glowed with a fire that never quite died - unless it was when, alone and unobserved, he took from his pocket a bit of buckskin in which was a silken tress of curling brown hair. Then his eyes shone with a light that was soft and luminous, and one seeing him then would have known that it was not a dream of gold that filled his heart , but of a brown-haired girl who had broken it.

On this day, the forenoon of the sixth since the agent had departed into the north, the end of the tense period of waiting was expected. Porcupine City had almost ceased to carry on the daily monotony of business. A score were lounging about the recorder's office. Women looked forth at frequent intervals through the open doors of the "city's" cabins, or gathered in two and threes to discuss this biggest sporting event ever known in the history of the town. Not a minute but scores of anxious eyes were turned searchingly up the river, down which the returning agent's canoe would first appear. With the dawn of this day O'Grady had refused to drink. He was stripped to the waist. His laugh was louder. Hatred as well as triumph glittered in his eyes, for to-day Jan Larose looked him coolly and squarely in the face, and nodded whenever he passed. It was almost noon when Jan spoke a few low words to his watchful Indian and walked to the top of the cedar-capped ridge that sheltered Porcupine City from the north winds.

From this ridge he could look straight into the north - the north where he was born. Only the Cree knew that for five nights he had slept, or sat awake, on the top of this ridge, with his face turned toward the polar star, and his heart breaking with loneliness and grief. Up there, far beyond where the green-topped forests and the sky seemed to meet, he could see a little cabin nestling under the stars - and Marie. Always his mind traveled back to the beginning of things, no matter how hard he tried to forget - even to the old days of years and years ago when he had toted the little Marie around on his back, and had crumpled her brown curls, and had revealed to her one by one the marvelous mysteries of the wilderness, with never a thought of the wonderful love that was to come. A half frozen little outcast brought in from the deep snows one day by Marie's father, he became first her playmate and brother - and after that lived in a few swift years of paradise and dreams. For Marie he had made of himself what he was. He had gone to Montreal. He had learned to read and write, he worked for the Company, he came to know the outside world, and at last the Government employed him. This was a triumph. He could still see the glow of pride and love in Marie's beautiful eyes when he came home after those two years in the great city. The Government sent for him each autumn after that. Deep into the wilderness he led the men who made the red and black lined maps. It was he who blazed out the northern limit of Banksian pine, and his name was in Government reports down in black and white - so that Marie and all the world could read.

One day he came back - and he found Clarry O'Grady at the Cummins' cabin. He had been there for a month with a broken leg. Perhaps it was the dangerous knowledge of the power of her beauty - the woman's instinct in her to tease with her prettiness, that led to Marie's flirtation with O'Grady. But Jan could not understand, and she played with fire - the fire of two hearts instead of one. The world went to pieces under Jan after that. There came the day when, in fair fight, he choked the taunting sneer from O'Grady's face back in the woods. He fought like a tiger, a mad demon. No one ever knew of that fight. And with the demon still raging in his breast he faced the girl. He could never quite remember what he had said. But it was terrible - and came straight from his soul. Then he went out, leaving Marie standing there white and silent. He did not go back. He had sworn never to do that, and during the weeks that followed it spread about that Marie Cummins had turned down Jan Larose, and that Clarry O'Grady was now the lucky man. It was one of the unexplained tricks of fate that had brought them together, and had set their discovery stakes side by side on Pelican Creek.

To-day, in spite of his smiling coolness, Jan's heart rankled with a bitterness that seemed to be concentrated of all the dregs that had ever entered into his life. It poisoned him, heart and soul. He was not a coward. He was not afraid of O'Grady.

And yet he knew that fate had already played the cards against him. He would lose. He was almost confident of that, even while he nerved himself to fight. There was the drop of savage superstition in him, and he told himself that something would happen to beat him out. O'Grady had gone into the home that was almost his own and had robbed him of Marie. In that fight in the forest he should have killed him. That would have been justice, as he knew it. But he had relented, half for Marie's sake, and half because he hated to take a human life, even though it were O'Grady's. But this time there would be no relenting. He had come alone to the top of the ridge to settle the last doubts with himself. Whoever won out, there would be a fight. It would be a magnificent fight, like that which his grandfather had fought and won for the honor of a woman years and years ago. He was even glad that O'Grady was trying to rob him of what he had searched for and found. There would be twice the justice in killing him now. And it would be done fairly, as his grandfather had done it.

Suddenly there came a piercing shout from the direction of the river, followed by a wild call for him through Jackpine's moose-horn. He answered the Cree's signal with a yell and tore down through the bush. When he reached the foot of the ridge at the edge of the clearing he saw the men, women and children of Porcupine City running to the river. In front of the recorder's office stood Jackpine, bellowing through his horn. O'Grady and his Indian were already shoving their canoe out into the stream, and even as he looked there came a break in the line of excited spectators, and through it hurried the agent toward the recorder's cabin.

Side by side, Jan and his Indian ran to their canoe. Jackpine was stripped to the waist, like O'Grady and his Chippewayan. Jan threw off only his caribou-skin coat. His dark woolen shirt was sleeveless, and his long slim arms, as hard as ribbed steel, were free. Half the crowd followed him. He smiled, and waved his hand, the dark pupils of his eyes shining big and black. Their canoe shot out until it was within a dozen yards of the other, and those ashore saw him laugh into O'Grady's sullen, set face. He was cool. Between smiling lips his white teeth gleamed, and the women stared with brighter eyes and flushed cheeks, wondering how Marie Cummins could have given up this man for the giant hulk and drink-reddened face of his rival. Those among the men who had wagered heavily against him felt a misgiving. There was something in Jan's smile that was more than coolness, and it was not bravado. Even as he smiled ashore, and spoke in low Cree to Jackpine, he felt at the belt that he had hidden under the caribou-skin coat. There were two sheaths there, and two knives, exactly alike. It was thus that his grandfather had set forth one summer day to avenge a wrong, nearly seventy years before.

The agent had entered the cabin, and now he reappeared, wiping his sweating face with a big red handkerchief. The recorder followed. He paused at the edge of the stream and made a megaphone of his hands.

"Gentlemen," he cried raucously, "both claims have been thrown out!"

A wild yell came from O'Grady. In a single flash four paddles struck the water, and the two canoes shot bow and bow up the stream toward the lake above the bend. The crowd ran even with them until the low swamp at the lake's edge stopped them. In that distance neither had gained a yard advantage. But there was a curious change of sentiment among those who returned to Porcupine City. That night betting was no longer two and three to one on O'Grady. It was even money.

For the last thing that the men of Porcupine City had seen was that cold, quiet smile of Jan Larose, the gleam of his teeth, the something in his eyes that is more to be feared among men than bluster and brute strength. They laid it to confidence. None guessed that this race held for Jan no thought of the gold at the end. None guessed that he was following out the working of a code as old as the name of his race in the north.

As the canoes entered the lake the smile left Jan's face. His lips tightened until they were almost a straight line. His eyes grew darker, his breath came more quickly. For a little while O'Grady's canoe drew steadily ahead of them, and when Jackpine's strokes went deeper and more powerful Jan spoke to him in Cree, and guided the canoe so that it cut straight as an arrow in O'Grady's wake. There was an advantage in that. It was small, but Jan counted on the cumulative results of good generalship.

His eyes never for an instant left O'Grady's huge, naked back. Between his knees lay his .303 rifle. He had figured on the fraction of time it would take him to drop his paddle, pick up the gun, and fire. This was his second point in generalship - getting the drop on O'Grady.

Once or twice in the first half hour O'Grady glanced back over his shoulder, and it was Jan who now laughed tauntingly at the other. There was something in that laugh that sent a chill through O'Grady. It was as hard as steel, a sort of madman's laugh.

It was seven miles to the first portage, and there were nine in the eighty-mile stretch. O'Grady and his Chippewayan were a hundred yards ahead when the prow of their canoe touched shore. They were a hundred and fifty ahead when both canoes were once more in the water on the other side of the portage, and O'Grady sent back a hoarse shout of triumph. Jan hunched himself a little lower. He spoke to Jackpine - and the race began. Swifter and swifter the canoes cut through the water. From five miles an hour to six, from six to six and a half - seven - seven and a quarter, and then the strain told. A paddle snapped in O'Grady's hands with a sound like a pistol shot. A dozen seconds were lost while he snatched up a new paddle and caught the Chippewayan's stroke, and Jan swung close into their wake again. At the end of the fifteenth mile, where the second portage began, O'Grady was two hundred yards in the lead. He gained another twenty on the portage and with a breath that was coming now in sobbing swiftness Jan put every ounce of strength behind the thrust of his paddle. Slowly they gained. Foot by foot, yard by yard, until for a third time they cut into O'Grady's wake. A dull pain crept into Jan's back. He felt it slowly creeping into his shoulders and to his arms. He looked at Jackpine and saw that he was swinging his body more and more with the motion of his arms. And then he saw that the terrific pace set by O'Grady was beginning to tell on the occupants of the canoe ahead. The speed grew less and less, until it was no more than seventy yards. In spite of the pains that were eating at his strength like swimmer's cramp, Jan could not restrain a low cry of exultation. O'Grady had planned to beat him out in that first twenty-mile spurt. And he had failed! His heart leaped with new hope even while his strokes were growing weaker.

Ahead of them, at the far end of the lake, there loomed up the black spruce timber which marked the beginning of the third portage, thirty miles from Porcupine City. Jan knew that he would win there - that he would gain an eighth of a mile in the half-mile carry. He knew of a shorter cut than that of the regular trail. He had cleared it himself, for he had spent a whole winter on that portage trapping lynx.

Marie lived only twelve miles beyond. More than once Marie had gone with him over the old trap line. She had helped him to plan the little log cabin he had built for himself on the edge of the big swamp, hidden away from all but themselves. It was she who had put the red paper curtains over the windows, and who, one day, had written on the corner of one of them: "My beloved Jan." He forgot O'Grady as he thought of Marie and those old days of happiness and hope. It was Jackpine who recalled him at last to what was happening. In amazement he saw that O'Grady and his Chippewayan had ceased paddling. They passed a dozen yards abreast of them. O'Grady's great arms and shoulders were glistening with perspiration. His face was purplish. In his eyes and on his lips was the old taunting sneer. He was panting like a wind-broken animal. As Jan passed he uttered no word.

An eighth of a mile ahead was the point where the regular portage began, but Jan swung around this into a shallow inlet from which his own secret trail was cut. Not until he was ashore did he look back. O'Grady and his Indian were paddling in a leisurely manner toward the head of the point. For a moment it looked as though they had given up the race, and Jan's heart leaped exultantly. O'Grady saw him and waved his hand. Then he jumped out to his knees in the water and the Chippewayan followed him. He shouted to Jan, and pointed down at the canoe. The next instant, with a powerful shove, he sent the empty birchbark speeding far out into the open water.

Jan caught his breath. He heard Jackpine's cry of amazement behind him. Then he saw the two men start on a swift run over the portage trail, and with a fierce, terrible cry he sprang toward his rifle, which he had leaned against a tree.

In that moment he would have fired, but O'Grady and the Indian had disappeared into the timber. He understood - O'Grady had tricked him, as he had tricked him in other ways. He had a second canoe waiting for him at the end of the portage, and perhaps others farther on. It was unfair. He could still hear O'Grady's taunting laughter as it had rung out in

Porcupine City, and the mystery of it was solved. His blood grew hot - so hot that his eyes burned, and his breath seemed to parch his lips. In that short space in which he stood paralyzed and unable to act his brain blazed like a volcano. Who - was helping O'Grady by having a canoe ready for him at the other side of the portage? He knew that no man had gone North from Porcupine City during those tense days of waiting. The code which all understood had prohibited that. Who, then, could it be? - who but Marie herself! In some way O'Grady had got word to her, and it was the Cummins' canoe that was waiting for him!

With a strange cry Jan lifted the bow of the canoe to his shoulder and led Jackpine in a run. His strength had returned. He did not feel the whiplike sting of boughs that struck him across the face. He scarcely looked at the little cabin of logs when they passed it. Deep down in his heart he called upon the Virgin to curse those two - Marie Cummins and Clarry O'Grady, the man and the girl who had cheated him out of love, out of home, out of everything he had possessed, and who were beating him now through perfidy and trickery.

His face and his hands were scratched and bleeding when they came to the narrow waterway, half lake and half river, which let into the Blind Loon. Another minute and they were racing again through the water. From the mouth of the channel he saw O'Grady and the Chippewayan a quarter of a mile ahead. Five miles beyond them was the fourth portage. It was hidden now by a thick pall of smoke rising slowly into the clear sky. Neither Jan nor the Indian had caught the pungent odors of burning forests in the air, and they knew that it was a fresh fire. Never in the years that Jan could remember had that portage been afire, and he wondered if this was another trick of O'Grady's. The fire spread rapidly as they advanced. It burst forth in a dozen places along the shore of the lake, sending up huge volumes of black smoke riven by lurid tongues of flame. O'Grady and his canoe became less and less distinct. Finally they disappeared entirely in the lowering clouds of the conflagration. Jan's eyes searched the water as they approached shore, and at last he saw what he had expected to find - O'Grady's empty canoe drifting slowly away from the beach. O'Grady and the Chippewayan were gone.

Over that half-mile portage Jan staggered with his eyes half closed and his breath coming in gasps. The smoke blinded him, and at times the heat of the fire scorched his face. In several places it had crossed the trail, and the hot embers burned through their moccasins. Once Jackpine uttered a cry of pain. But Jan's lips were set. Then, above the roar of the flames sweeping down upon the right of them, he caught the low thunder of Dead Man's Whirlpool and the cataract that had made the portage necessary. From the heated earth their feet came to a narrow ledge of rock, worn smooth by the furred and moccasined tread of centuries, with the chasm on one side of them and a wall of rock on the other. Along the crest of that wall, a hundred feet above them, the fire swept in a tornado of flame and smoke. A tree crashed behind them, a dozen seconds too late. Then the trail widened and sloped down into the dip that ended the portage. For an instant Jan paused to get his bearing, and behind him Jackpine shouted a warning.

Up out of the smoldering oven where O'Grady should have found his canoe two men were rushing toward them. They were O'Grady and the Chippewayan. He caught the gleam of a knife in the Indian's hand. In O'Grady's there was something larger and darker - a club, and Jan dropped his end of the canoe with a glad cry, and drew one of the knives from his belt. Jackpine came to his side, with his hunting knife in his hand, measuring with glittering eyes the oncoming foe of his race - the Chippewayan.

And Jan laughed softly to himself, and his teeth gleamed again, for at last fate was playing his game. The fire had burned O'Grady's canoe, and it was to rob him of his own canoe that O'Grady was coming to fight. A canoe! He laughed again, while the fire roared over his head and the whirlpool thundered at his feet. O'Grady would fight for a canoe - for gold - while he - HE - would fight for something else, for the vengeance of a man whose soul and honor had been sold. He cared nothing for the canoe. He cared nothing for the gold. He told himself, in this one tense moment of waiting, that he cared no longer for Marie. It was the fulfillment of the code.

He was still smiling when O'Grady was so near that he could see the red glare in his eyes. There was no word, no shout, no sound of fury or defiance as the two men stood for an instant just out of striking distance. Jan heard the coming together of Jackpine and the Chippewayan. He heard them straggling, but not the flicker of an eyelash did his gaze leave O'Grady's face. Both men understood. This time had to come. Both had expected it, even from that day of the fight in the woods when fortune had favored Jan. The burned canoe had only hastened the hour a little. Suddenly Jan's free hand reached behind him to his belt. He drew forth the second knife and tossed it at O'Grady's feet.

O'Grady made a movement to pick it up, and then, while Jan was partly off his guard, came at him with a powerful swing of the club. It was his catlike quickness, the quickness almost of the great northern loon that evades a rifle ball, that had won for Jan in the forest fight. It saved him now. The club cut through the air over his head, and, carried by the momentum of his own blow, O'Grady lurched against him with the full force of his two hundred pounds of muscle and bone. Jan's knife swept in an upward flash and plunged to the hilt through the flesh of his enemy's forearm. With a cry of pain O'Grady dropped his club, and the two crashed to the stone floor of the trail. This was the attack that Jan had feared and tried to foil, and with a lightning-like squirming movement he swung himself half free, and on his back, with O'Grady's huge hands linking at his throat, he drew back his knife arm for the fatal plunge.

In this instant, so quick that he could scarcely have taken a breath in the time, his eyes took in the other struggle between Jackpine and the Chippewayan. The two Indians had locked themselves in a deadly embrace. All thought of masters, of life or death, were forgotten in the roused-up hatred that fired them now in their desire to kill. They had drawn close to the edge of the chasm. Under them the thundering roar of the whirlpool was unheard, their ears caught no sound of the moaning surge of the flames far over their heads. Even as Jan stared horror-stricken in that one moment, they locked at the edge of the chasm. Above the tumult of the flood below and the fire above there rose a wild yell, and the two plunged down into the abyss, locked and fighting even as they fell in a twisting, formless shape to the death below.

It happened in an instant - like the flash of a quick picture on a screen - and even as Jan caught the last of Jackpine's terrible face, his hand drove eight inches of steel toward O'Grady's body. The blade struck something hard - something that was neither bone nor flesh, and he drew back again to strike. He had struck the steel buckle on O'Grady's belt. This time -

A sudden hissing roar filled the air. Jan knew that he did not strike - but he scarcely knew more than that in the first shock of the fiery avalanche that had dropped upon them from the rock wall of the mountain. He was conscious of fighting desperately to drag himself from under a weight that was not O'Grady's - a weight that stifled the breath in his lungs, that crackled in his ears, that scorched his face and his hands, and was burning out his eyes. A shriek rang in his ears unlike any other cry of man he had ever heard, and he knew that it was O'Grady's. He pulled himself out, foot by foot, until fresher air struck his nostrils, and dragged himself nearer and nearer to the edge of the chasm. He could not rise. His limbs were paralyzed. His knife arm dragged at his side. He opened his eyes and found that he could see. Where they had fought was the smoldering ruin of a great tree, and standing out of the ruin of that tree, half naked, his hands tearing wildly at his face, was O'Grady. Jan's fingers clutched at a small rock. He called out, but there was no meaning to the sound he made. Clarry O'Grady threw out his great arms.

"Jan - Jan Larose - " he cried. "My God, don't strike now! I'm blind - blind - "

He staggered back, as if expecting a blow. "Don't strike ! " he almost shrieked. "Mother of Heaven - my eyes are burned out - I'm blind - blind - "

He backed to the wall, his huge form crouched, his hands reaching out as if to ward off the deathblow. Jan tried to move, and the effort brought a groan of agony to his lips. A second crash filled his ears as a second avalanche of fiery debris plunged down upon the trail farther back. He stared straight up through the stifling smoke. Lurid tongues of flame were leaping over the wall of the mountain where the edge of the forest was enveloped in a sea of twisting and seething fire. It was only a matter of minutes - perhaps seconds. Death had them both in its grip.

He looked again at O'Grady, and there was no longer the desire for the other's life in his heart. He could see that the giant was unharmed, except for his eyes.

"Listen, O'Grady," he cried. "My legs are broken, I guess, and I can't move. It's sure death to stay here another minute. You can get away. Follow the wall - to your right. The slope is still free of fire, and - and - "

O'Grady began to move, guiding himself slowly along the wall. Then, suddenly, he stopped.

"Jan Larose - you say you can't move?" he shouted.

"Yes."

Slowly O'Grady turned and came gropingly toward the sound of Jan's voice. Jan held tight to the rock that he had gripped in his left hand. Was it possible that O'Grady would kill him now, stricken as he was? He tried to drag himself to a new position, but his effort was futile.

"Jan! Jan Larose!" called O'Grady, stopping to listen.

Jan held his breath. Then the truth seemed to dawn upon O'Grady. He laughed, differently than he had laughed before, and stretched out his arms.

"My God, Jan," he cried, "you don't think I'm clean BEAST, do you? The fight's over, man, an' I guess God A'mighty brought this on us to show what fools we was. Where are y', Jan Larose? I'm goin' t' carry you out!"

"I'm here!" called Jan.

He could see truth and fearlessness in O'Grady's sightless face, and he guided him without fear. Their hands met. Then O'Grady lowered himself and hoisted Jan to his shoulders as easily as he would have lifted a boy. He straightened himself and drew a deep breath, broken by a stabbing throb of pain.

"I'm blind an' I won't see any more," he said, "an' mebbe you won't ever walk any more. But if we ever git to that gold I kin do the work and you kin show me how. Now - p'int out the way, Jan Larose!"

With his arms clasped about O'Grady's naked shoulders, Jan's smarting eyes searched through the thickening smother of fire and smoke for a road that the other's feet might tread. He shouted "Left" - "right" - "right" - "right" - "left" into this blind companion's ears until they touched the wall. As the heat smote them more fiercely, O'Grady bowed his great head upon his chest and obeyed mutely the signals that rang in his ears. The bottoms of his moccasins were burned from his feet, live embers ate at his flesh, his broad chest was a fiery blister, and yet he strode on straight into the face of still greater heat and greater torture, uttering no sound that could be heard above the steady roar of the flames. And Jan, limp and helpless on his back, felt then the throb and pulse of a giant life under him, the straining of thick neck, of massive shoulders and the grip of powerful arms whose strength told him that at last he had found the comrade and the man in Clarry O'Grady. "Right" - "left" - "left" - "right" he shouted, and then he called for O'Grady to stop in a voice that was shrill with warning.

"There's fire ahead," he yelled. "We can't follow the wall any longer. There's an open space close to the chasm. We can make that, but there's only about a yard to spare. Take short steps - one step each time I tell you. Now - left - left - left - left - "

Like a soldier on drill, O'Grady kept time with his scorched feet until Jan turned him again to face the storm of fire, while one of his own broken legs dangled over the abyss into which Jackpine and the Chippewayan had plunged to their death. Behind them, almost where they had fought, there crashed down a third avalanche from the edge of the mountain. Not a shiver ran through O'Grady's great body. Steadily and unflinchingly - step - step - step - he went ahead, while the last threads of his moccasins smoked and burned. Jan could no longer see half a dozen yards in advance. A wall of black smoke rose in their faces, and he pulled O'Grady's ear:

"We've got just one chance, Clarry. I can't see any more. Keep straight ahead - and run for it, and may the good God help us now!"

And Clarry O'Grady, drawing one great breath that was half fire into his lungs, ran straight into the face of what looked like death to Jan Larose. In that one moment Jan closed his eyes and waited for the plunge over the cliff. But in place of death a sweep of air that seemed almost cold struck his face, and he opened his eyes to find the clear and uncharred slope leading before them down to the edge of the lake. He shouted the news into O'Grady's ear, and then there arose from O'Grady's chest a great sobbing cry, partly of joy, partly of pain, and more than all else of that terrible grief which came of the knowledge that back in the pit of death from which he had escaped he had left forever the vision of life itself. He dropped Jan in the edge of the water, and, plunging in to his waist, he threw handful after handful of water into his own swollen face, and then stared upward, as though this last experiment was also his last hope.

"My God, I'm blind - stone blind!"

Jan was staring hard into O'Grady's face. He called him nearer, took the swollen and blackened face between his two hands, and his voice was trembling with joy when he spoke.

"You're not blind - not for good - O'Grady," he said. "I've seen men like you before - twice. You - you'll get well. O'Grady - Clarry O'Grady - let's shake! I'm a brother to you from this day on. And I'm glad - glad – that Marie loves a man like you!"

O'Grady had gripped his hand, but he dropped it now as though it had been one of the live brands that had hurtled down upon them from the top of the mountain.

"Marie - man - why - she HATES me!" he cried. "It's you - YOU - Jan Larose, that she loves! I went there with a broken leg, an' I fell in love with her. But she wouldn't so much as let me touch her hand, an' she talked of you - always - always - until I had learned to hate you before you came. I dunno why she did it - that other thing - unless it was to make you jealous. I guess it was all f'r fun, Jan. She didn't know. The day you went away she sent me after you. But I hated you - hated you worse'n she hated me. It's you - you - "

He clutched his hands at his sightless face again, and suddenly Jan gave a wild shout. Creeping around the edge of a smoking headland, he had caught sight of a man and a canoe.

"There's a man in a canoe!" he cried, "He sees us! O'Grady - "

He tried to lift himself, but fell back with a groan. Then he laughed, and, in spite of his agony, there was a quivering happiness in his voice.

"He's coming, O'Grady. And it looks - it looks like a canoe we both know. We'll go back to her cabin together, O'Grady. And when we're on our legs again - well, I never wanted the gold. That's yours - all of it."

A determined look had settled in O'Grady's face. He groped his way to Jan's side, and their hands met in a clasp that told more than either could have expressed of the brotherhood and strength of men.

"You can't throw me off like that, Jan Larose," he said. "We're pardners!"

THE MATCH

Sergeant Brokaw was hatchet-faced, with shifting pale blue eyes that had a glint of cruelty in them. He was tall, and thin, and lithe as a cat. He belonged to the Royal Northwest Mounted Police, and was one of the best men on the trail that had ever gone into the North. His business was man hunting. Ten years of seeking after human prey had given to him many of the characteristics of a fox. For six of those ten years he had represented law north of fifty-three. Now he had come to the end of his last hunt, close up to the Arctic Circle. For one hundred and eighty-seven days he had been following a man. The hunt had begun in midsummer, and it was now midwinter. Billy Loring, who was wanted for murder, had been a hard man to find. But he was caught at last, and Brokaw was keenly exultant. It was his greatest achievement. It would mean a great deal for him down at headquarters.

In the rough and dimly lighted cabin his man sat opposite him, on a bench, his manacled hands crossed over his knees. He was a younger man than Brokaw - thirty, or a little better. His hair was long, reddish, and untrimmed. A stubble of reddish beard covered his face. His eyes, too, were blue - of the deep, honest blue that one remembers, and most frequently trusts. He did not look like a criminal. There was something almost boyish in his face, a little hollowed by long privation.

James Oliver Curwood

He was the sort of man that other men liked. Even Brokaw, who had a heart like flint in the face of crime, had melted a little.

"Ugh!" he shivered. "Listen to that beastly wind! It means three days of storm." Outside a gale was blowing straight down from the Arctic. They could hear the steady moaning of it in the spruce tops over the cabin, and now and then there came one of those raging blasts that filled the night with strange shrieking sounds. Volleys of fine, hard snow beat against the one window with a rattle like shot. In the cabin it was comfortable. It was Billy's cabin. He had built it deep in a swamp, where there were lynx and fisher cat to trap, and where he had thought that no one could find him. The sheet-iron stove was glowing hot. An oil lamp hung from the ceiling. Billy was sitting so that the glow of this fell in his face. It scintillated on the rings of steel about his wrists. Brokaw was a cautious man, as well as a clever one, and he took no chances.

"I like storms - when you're inside, an' close to a stove," replied Billy. "Makes me feel sort of - safe." He smiled a little grimly. Even at that it was not an unpleasant smile.

Brokaw's snow-reddened eyes gazed at the other.

"There's something in that," he said. "This storm will give you at least three days more of life."

"Won't you drop that?" asked the prisoner, turning his face a little, so that it was shaded from the light.

"You've got me now, an' I know what's coming as well as you do." His voice was low and quiet, with the faintest trace of a broken note in it, deep down in his throat. "We're alone, old man, and a long way from anyone. I ain't blaming you for catching me. I haven't got anything against you. So let's drop this other thing - what I'm going down to – and talk something pleasant. I know I'm going to hang. That's the law. It'll be pleasant enough when it comes, don't you think? Let's talk about - about - home. Got any kids?"

Brokaw shook his head, and took his pipe from his mouth.

"Never married," he said shortly.

"Never married," mused Billy, regarding him with a curious softening of his blue eyes. "You don't know what you've missed, Brokaw. Of course, it's none of my business, but you've got a home - somewhere - "
Brokaw shook his head again.

"Been in the service ten years," he said. "I've got a mother living with my brother somewhere down in York State. I've sort of lost track of them. Haven't seen 'em in five years."

Billy was looking at him steadily. Slowly he rose to his feet, lifted his manacled hands, and turned down the light.

"Hurts my eyes," he said, and he laughed frankly as he caught the suspicious glint in Brokaw's eyes. He seated himself again, and leaned over toward the other. "I haven't talked to a white man for three months," he added, a little hesitatingly. "I've been hiding - close. I had a dog for a time, and he died, an' I didn't dare go hunting for another. I knew you fellows were pretty

James Oliver Curwood

close after me. But I wanted to get enough fur to take me to South America. Had it all planned, an' SHE was going to join me there - with the kid. Understand? If you'd kept away another month - "

There was a husky break in his voice, and he coughed to clear it.

"You don't mind if I talk, do you - about her, an' the kid? I've got to do it, or bust, or go mad. I've got to because - to-day - she was twenty-four - at ten o'clock in the morning - an' it's our wedding day - "

The half gloom hid from Brokaw what was in the other's face. And then Billy laughed almost joyously. "Say, but she's been a true little pardner," he whispered proudly, as there came a lull in the storm. "She was just born for me, an' everything seemed to happen on her birthday, an' that's why I can't be downhearted even NOW. It's her birthday? You see, an' this morning, before you came, I was just that happy that I set a plate for her at the table, an' put her picture and a curl of her hair beside it - set the picture up so it was looking at me - an' we had breakfast together. Look here - "

He moved to the table, with Brokaw watching him like a cat, and brought something back with him, wrapped in a soft piece of buckskin. He unfolded the buckskin tenderly, and drew forth a long curl that rippled a dull red and gold in the lamp-glow, and then he handed a photograph to Brokaw.

"That's her!" he whispered.

Brokaw turned so that the light fell on the picture. A sweet , girlish face smiled at him from out of a wealth of flowing, disheveled curls.

"She had it taken that way just for me," explained
Billy, with the enthusiasm of a boy in his voice. "She's
always wore her hair in curls - an' a braid - for me,
when we're home. I love it that way. Guess I may be
silly but I'll tell you why. THAT was down in York
State, too. She lived in a cottage, all grown over with
honeysuckle an' morning glory, with green hills and
valleys all about it - and the old apple orchard just
behind. That day we were in the orchard, all red an'
white with bloom, and she dared me to a race. I let her
beat me, and when I came up she stood under one of
the trees, her cheeks like the pink blossoms, and her
hair all tumbled about her like an armful of gold,
shaking the loose apple blossoms down on her head. I
forgot everything then, and I didn't stop until I had her
in my arms, an' - an' she's been my little pardner ever
since. After the baby came we moved up into Canada,
where I had a good chance in a new mining town. An'
then - " A furious blast of the storm sent the
overhanging spruce tops smashing against the top of
the cabin. Straight overhead the wind shrieked almost
like human voices, and the one window rattled as
though it were shaken by human hands. The lamp had
been burning lower and lower. It began to flicker now,
the quick sputter of the wick lost in the noise of the
gale. Then it went out. Brokaw leaned over and opened
the door of the big box stove, and the red glow of the
fire took the place of the lamplight. He leaned back
and relighted his pipe, eyeing Billy. The sudden blast,
the going out of the light, the opening of the stove
door, had all happened in a minute, but the interval
was long enough to bring a change in Billy's voice. It
was cold and hard when he continued. He leaned
over toward Brokaw , and the boyishness had gone

from his face.

"Of course, I can't expect you to have any sympathy for this other business, Brokaw," he went on. "Sympathy isn't in your line, an' you wouldn't be the big man you are in the service if you had it. But I'd like to know what YOU would have done. We were up there six months, and we'd both grown to love the big woods, and she was growing prettier and happier every day - when Thorne, the new superintendent, came up. One day she told me that she didn't like Thorne, but I didn't pay much attention to that, and laughed at her, and said he was a good fellow. After that I could see that something was worrying her, and pretty soon I couldn't help from seeing what it was, and everything came out. It was Thorne. He was persecuting her. She hadn't told me, because she knew it would make trouble and I'd lose my job. One afternoon I came home earlier than usual, and found her crying. She put her arms round my neck, and just cried it all out, with her face snuggled in my neck, and kissin' me - "

Brokaw could see the cords in Billy's neck. His manacled hands were clenched.

"What would you have done, Brokaw?" he asked huskily. "What if you had a wife, an' she told you that another man had insulted her, and was forcing his attentions on her, and she asked you to give up your job and take her away? Would you have done it, Brokaw? No, you wouldn't. You'd have hunted up the man. That's what I did. He had been drinking - just enough to make him devilish, and he laughed at me - I didn't mean to strike so hard. - But it happened. I killed him. I got away. She and the baby are down in the little cottage again - down in York State - an' I know she's awake this minute - our wedding day - thinking of me, an' praying for me, and counting the days between now and spring. We were going to South America then."

Brokaw rose to his feet, and put fresh wood into the stove.

"I guess it must be pretty hard," he said, straightening himself. "But the law up here doesn't take them things into account - not very much. It may let you off with manslaugher - ten or fifteen years. I hope it does. Let's turn in."

Billy stood up beside him. He went with Brokaw to a bunk built against the wall, and the sergeant drew a fine steel chain from his pocket. Billy lay down, his hands crossed over his breast, and Brokaw deftly fastened the chain about his ankles.

"And I suppose you think THIS is hard, too," he added. "But I guess you'd do it if you were me. Ten years of this sort of work learns you not to take chances. If you want anything in the night just whistle." It had been a hard day with Brokaw, and he slept soundly. For an hour Billy lay awake, thinking of home, and listening to the wail of the storm. Then he, too, fell into sleep - a restless, uneasy slumber filled with troubled visions. For a time there had come a lull in the storm, but now it broke over the cabin with increased fury. A hand seemed slapping at the window, threatening to break it. The spruce boughs moaned and twisted overhead, and a volley of wind and snow shot suddenly down the chimney, forcing open the stove door, so that a shaft of ruddy light cut like a red knife through the dense gloom of the cabin. In varying ways the sounds played a part in Billy's dreams. In all those dreams, and segments of dreams, the girl - his wife - was present. Once they had gone for wild flowers and had been caught in a thunderstorm, and had run to an old and disused barn in the middle of a field for shelter. He was back in that barn again, with HER - and he could feel her trembling against him, and he was stroking her hair, as the thunder crashed over them and the lightning filled her eyes with fear. After that there came to him a vision of the early autumn nights when they had gone corn roasting, with other young people. He had always been afflicted with a slight nasal trouble, and smoke irritated him. It set him sneezing, and kept him dodging about the fire, and she had always laughed when the smoke persisted in following him about, like a young scamp of a boy bent on tormenting him. The smoke was unusually persistent to-night. He tossed in his bunk, and buried his face in the blanket that answered for a pillow. The smoke reached him even there, and he sneezed chokingly. In that instant the girl's face disappeared. He sneezed again - and awoke.

A startled gasp broke from his lips, and the handcuffs about his wrists clanked as he raised his hands to his face. In that moment his dazed senses adjusted themselves. The cabin was full of smoke. It partly blinded him, but through it he could see tongues of fire shooting toward the ceiling. He could hear the crackling of burning pitch, and he yelled wildly to Brokaw. In an instant the sergeant was on his feet. He rushed to the table, where he had placed a pail of water the evening before, and Billy heard the hissing of the water as it struck the flaming wall.

"Never mind that," he shouted. "The shack's built of pitch cedar. We've got to get out!" Brokaw groped his way to him through the smoke and began fumbling at the chain about his ankles.

"I can't - find - the key - " he gasped chokingly. "Here grab hold of me!"

He caught Billy under the arms and dragged him to the door. As he opened it the wind came in with a rush and behind them the whole cabin burst into a furnace of flame. Twenty yards from the cabin he dropped Billy in the snow, and ran back. In that seething room of smoke and fire was everything on which their lives depended, food, blankets, even their coats and caps and snowshoes. But he could go no farther than the door. He returned to Billy, found the key in his pocket, and freed him from the chain about his ankles. Billy stood up. As he looked at Brokaw the glass in the window broke and a sea of flame sprouted through. It lighted up their faces. The sergeant's jaw was set hard. His leathery face was curiously white. He could not keep from shivering. There was a strange smile on Billy's face, and a strange look in his eyes. Neither of the two men had undressed for sleep, but their coats, and caps, and heavy mittens were in the flames.

Billy rattled his handcuffs. Brokaw looked him squarely in the eyes.

"You ought to know this country," he said. "What'll we do?"

"The nearest post is sixty miles from here," said Billy.

"I know that," replied Brokaw. "And I know that Thoreau's cabin is only twenty miles from here. There must be some trapper or Indian shack nearer than that.

Is there?" In the red glare of the fire Billy smiled. His teeth gleamed at Brokaw. It was a lull of the wind, and he went close to Brokaw, and spoke quietly, his eyes shining more and more with that strange light that had come into them.

"This is going to be a big sight easier than hanging, or going to jail for half my life, Brokaw - an' you don't think I'm going to be fool enough to miss the chance, do you? It ain't hard to die of cold. I've almost been there once or twice. I told you last night why I couldn't give up hope - that something good for me always came on her birthday, or near to it. An' it's come. It's forty below, an' we won't live the day out. We ain't got a mouthful of grub. We ain't got clothes enough on to keep us from freezing inside the shanty, unless we had a fire. Last night I saw you fill your match bottle and put it in your coat pocket. Why, man, WE AIN'T EVEN GOT A MATCH!"

In his voice there was a thrill of triumph. Brokaw's hands were clenched, as if some one had threatened to strike him.

"You mean - " he gasped.

"Just this," interrupted Billy, and his voice was harder than Brokaw's now. "The God you used to pray to when you was a kid has given me a choice, Brokaw, an' I'm going to take it. If we stay by this fire, an' keep it up, we won't die of cold, but of starvation. We'll be dead before we get half way to Thoreau's. There's an Indian shack that we could make, but you'll never find it - not unless you unlock these irons and give me that revolver at your belt. Then I'll take you over there as my prisoner. That'll give me another chance for South

America - an' the kid an' home." Brokaw was buttoning the thick collar of his shirt close up about his neck. On his face, too, there came for a moment a grim and determined smile.

"Come on," he said, "we'll make Thoreau's or die."

"Sure," said Billy, stepping quickly to his side. "I suppose I might lie down in the snow, an' refuse to budge. I'd win my game then, wouldn't I? But we'll play it - on the square. It's Thoreau's, or die. And it's up to you to find Thoreau's."

He looked back over his shoulder at the burning cabin as they entered the edge of the forest, and in the gray darkness that was preceding dawn he smiled to himself. Two miles to the south, in a thick swamp, was Indian Joe's cabin. They could have made it easily. On their way to Thoreau's they would pass within a mile of it. But Brokaw would never know. And they would never reach Thoreau's. Billy knew that. He looked at the man hunter as he broke trail ahead of him - at the pugnacious hunch of his shoulders, his long stride, the determined clench of his hands, and wondered what the soul and the heart of a man like this must be, who in such an hour would not trade life for life. For almost three-quarters of an hour Brokaw did not utter a word. The storm had broke. Above the spruce tops the sky began to clear. Day came slowly. And it was growing steadily colder. The swing of Brokaw'a arms and shoulders kept the blood in them circulating, while Billy's manacled wrists held a part of his body almost rigid. He knew that his hands were already frozen. His arms were numb, and when at last Brokaw paused for a moment on the edge of a frozen stream Billy thrust out his hands, and clanked the steel rings.

"It must be getting colder," he said. "Look at that."

The cold steel had seared his wrists like hot iron, and had pulled off patches of skin and flesh. Brokaw looked, and hunched his shoulders. His lips were blue. His cheeks, ears, and nose were frost-bitten. There was a curious thickness in his voice when he spoke.

"Thoreau lives on this creek," he said. "How much farther is it?"

"Fifteen or sixteen miles," replied Billy. "You'll last just about five, Brokaw. I won't last that long unless you take these things off and give me the use of my arms."

"To knock out my brains when I ain't looking," growled Brokaw. "I guess - before long - you'll be willing to tell where the Indian's shack is." He kicked his way through a drift of snow to the smoother surface of the stream. There was a breath of wind in their faces, and Billy bowed his head to it. In the hours of his greatest loneliness and despair Billy had kept up his fighting spirit by thinking of pleasant things, and now, as he followed in Brokaw's trail, he began to think of home. It was not hard for him to bring up visions of the girl wife who would probably never know how he had died. He forgot Brokaw. He followed in the trail mechanically, failing to notice that his captor's pace was growing steadily slower, and that his own feet were dragging more and more like leaden weights. He was back among the old hills again, and the sun was shining, and he heard laughter and song. He saw Jeanne standing at the gate in front of the little white cottage, smiling at him, and waving Baby Jeanne's tiny hand at him as he looked back over his shoulder from down the dusty road. His mind did not often travel as far as the mining camp, and he had completely forgotten it now. He no longer felt the sting and pain of the intense cold. It was Brokaw who brought him back into the reality of things. The sergeant stumbled and fell in a drift, and Billy fell over him. For a moment the two men sat half buried in the snow, looking at each other without speaking. Brokaw moved first. He rose to his feet with an effort. Billy made an attempt to follow him. After three efforts he gave it up, and blinked up into Brokaw's face with a queer laugh. The laugh was almost soundless. There had come a change in Brokaw's face. Its determination and confidence were gone. At last the iron mask of the Law was broken, and there shone through it something of the emotions and the brotherhood of man. He was fumbling in one of his pockets, and drew out the key to the handcuffs. It was a small key, and he held it between his stiffened fingers with diffic ulty. He knelt down beside Billy. The keyhole was filled with snow. It took a long time - ten minutes - before the key was fitted in and the lock clicked. He helped to tear off the cuffs. Billy felt no sensation as bits of skin and flesh came "with them. Brokaw gave him a hand, and assisted him to rise. For the first time he spoke.

"Guess you've got me beat, Billy," he said.

"Where's the Indian's?"

He drew his revolver from its holster and tossed it in the snowdrift. The shadow of a smile passed grimly over his face. Billy looked about him. They had stopped where the frozen path of a smaller stream joined the creek. He raised one of his stiffened arms and pointed to it.

James Oliver Curwood

"Follow that creek - four miles - and you'll come to Indian Joe's shack," he said.

"And a mile is just about our limit"

"Just about - your's," replied Billy. "I can't make another half. If we had a fire - "

"IF - " wheezed Brokaw.

"If we had a fire," continued Billy. "We could warm ourselves, an' make the Indian's shack easy, couldn't we?"

Brokaw did not answer. He had turned toward the creek when one of Billy's pulseless hands fell heavily on his arm.

"Look here, Brokaw."

Brokaw turned. They looked into each other's eyes.

"I guess mebby you're a man, Brokaw," said Billy quietly. "You've done what you thought was your duty. You've kept your word to th' law, an' I believe you'll keep your word with me. If I say the word that'll save us now will you go back to headquarters an' report me dead?" For a full half minute their eyes did not waver.

Then Brokaw said:

"No."

Billy dropped his hand. It was Brokaw's hand that fell on his arm now.

"I can't do that," he said. "In ten years I ain't run out the white flag once. It's something that ain't known in the service. There ain't a coward in it, or a man who's afraid to die. But I'll play you square. I'll wait until we're both on our feet, again, and then I'll give you twenty-four hours the start of me."

Billy was smiling now. His hand reached out. Brokaw's met it, and the two joined in a grip that their numb fingers scarcely felt.

"Do you know," said Billy softly, "there's been somethin' runnin' in my head ever since we left the burning cabin. It's something my mother taught me: 'Do unto others as you'd have others do unto you.' I'm a d - fool, ain't I? But I'm goin' to try the experiment, Brokaw, an' see what comes of it. I could drop in a snowdrift an' let you go on - to die. Then I could save myself. But I'm going to take your word - an' do the other thing. I'VE GOT A MATCH."

"A MATCH!"

"Just one. I remember dropping it in my pants pocket yesterday when I was out on the trail. It's in THIS pocket. Your hand is in better shape than mine. Get it."

Life had leaped into Brokaw's face. He thrust his hand into Billy's pocket, staring at him as he fumbled, as if fearing that he had lied. When he drew his hand out the match was between his fingers.

"Ah!" he whispered excitedly.

"Don't get nervous," warned Billy. "It's the only one."

Brokaw's eyes were searching the low timber along the shore. "There's a birch tree," he cried. "Hold it - while I gather a pile of bark!"

He gave the match to Billy, and staggered through the snow to the bank. Strip after strip of the loose bark he tore from the tree. Then he gathered it in a heap in the shelter of a low-hanging spruce, and added dry sticks, and still more bark, to it. When it was ready he stood with his hands in his pockets, and looked at Billy.

"If we had a stone, an' a piece of paper - " he began.

Billy thrust a hand that felt like lifeless lead inside his shirt, and fumbled in a pocket he had made there. Brokaw watched him with red, eager eyes. The hand reappeared, and in it was the buckskin wrapped photograph he had seen the night before, Billy took off the buckskin. About the picture there was a bit of tissue paper. He gave this and the match to Brokaw.

"There's a little gun-file in the pocket the match came from," he said. "I had it mending a trapchain. You can scratch the match on that."

He turned so that Brokaw could reach into the pocket, and the man hunter thrust in his hand. When he brought it forth he held the file. There was a smile on Billy's frostbitten face as he held the picture for a moment under Brokaw's eyes. Billy's own hands had ruffled up the girl's shining curls an instant before the picture was taken, and she was laughing at him when the camera clicked.

"It's all up to her, Brokaw," Billy said gently. "I told you that last night. It was she who woke me up before the fire got us. If you ever prayed - pray a little now. FOR SHE'S GOING TO STRIKE THAT MATCH!"

He still looked at the picture as Brokaw knelt beside the pile he had made. He heard the scratch of the match on the file, but his eyes did not turn. The living, breathing face of the most beautiful thing in the world was speaking to him from out of that picture. His mind was dazed. He swayed a little. He heard a voice, low and sweet, and so distant that it came to him like the faintest whisper. "I am coming - I am coming, Billy - coming - coming - coming - " A joyous cry surged up from his soul, but it died on his lips in a strange gasp. A louder cry brought him back to himself for a moment. It was from Brokaw. The sergeant's face was terrible to behold. He rose to his feet, swaying, his hands clutched at his breast. His voice was thick - hopeless.

"The match - went - out - " He staggered up to Billy, his eyes like a madman's. Billy swayed dizzily. He laughed, even as he crumpled down in the snow. As if in a dream he saw Brokaw stagger off on the frozen trail. He saw him disappear in his hopeless effort to reach the Indian's shack. And then a strange darkness closed him in, and in that darkness he heard still the sweet voice of his wife. It spoke his name again and again, and it urged him to wake up - wake up - WAKE UP! It seemed a long time before he could respond to it. But at last he opened his eyes. He dragged himself to his knees, and looked first to find Brokaw. But the man hunter had gone - forever. The picture was still in his hand. Less distinctly than before he saw the girl smiling at him. And then - at his back - he heard a strange and new sound. With an effort he turned to discover what it was.

The match had hidden an unseen spark from Brokaw's eyes. From out of the pile of fuel was rising a pillar of smoke and flame.

THE HONOR OF HER PEOPLE

"It ees not so much - What you call heem? - leegend, thees honor of the Beeg Snows!" said Jan softly.

He had risen to his feet and gazed placidly over the crackling box-stove into the eyes of the red-faced Englishman.

"Leegend is lie! Thees is truth!"

There was no lack of luster in the black eyes that roved inquiringly from the Englishman's bantering grin to the others in the room. Mukee, the half Cree, was sitting with his elbows on his knees gazing with stoic countenance at this new curiosity who had wandered four hundred miles northward from civilization. Williams, the Hudson's Bay man who claimed to be all white, was staring hard at the red side of the stove, and the factor's son looked silently at Jan. He and the half-breed noted the warm glow in the eyes that rested casually upon the Englishman.

"It ees truth - thees honor of the Beeg Snows!" said Jan again, and his moccasined feet fell in heavy, thumping tread to the door.

That was the first time he had spoken that evening, and not even the half Cree, or Williams, or the factor's son guessed how the blood was racing through his veins. Outside he stood with the pale, cold glow of the Aurora Borealis shining upon him, and the limitless wilderness, heavy in its burden of snow, reaching out into the ghost-gray fabric of the night. The Englishman's laugh followed him, boisterous and grossly thick, and Jan moved on, - wondering how much longer the half Cree and Williams and the factor's son would listen to the things that this man was saying of the most beautiful thing that had ever come into their lives.

"It ees truth, I swear, by dam' - thees honor of what he calls the 'Beeg Snows!'" persisted Jan to himself, and he set his back to the factor's office and trudged through the snow.

When he came to the black ledge of the spruce and balsam forest he stopped and looked back. It was an hour past bedtime at the post. The Company's store loomed up silent and lightless. The few log cabins betrayed no signs of life. Only in the factor's office, which was the Company's haven for the men of the wilderness, was there a waste of kerosene, and that was because of the Englishman whom Jan was beginning to hate. He stared back at the one glowing window with a queer thickening in his throat and a clenching of the hands in the pockets of his caribou-skin coat. Then he looked long and wistfully at a little cabin which stood apart from the rest, and to himself he whispered again what he had said to the Englishman. Until to-night - or, perhaps, until two weeks ago - Jan had been satisfied with his world. It was a big, passionless world, mostly of snow and ice and endless privation, but he loved it, and there was only a fast-fading memory of another world in his brain. It was a world of big, honest hearts kept warm within caribou skins, of moccasined men whom endless solitude had taught to say little and do much - a world of "Big Snows," as the Englishman had said, in which Jan and all his people had come very close to the things which God created. Without the steely gray flash of those mystery-lights over the Arctic pole Jan would have been homesick; his soul would have withered and died in anything but this wondrous land which he knew, with its billion dazzling stars by night and its eye-blinding brilliancy by day. For Jan, in a way, was fortunate. He had in him an infinitesimal measure of the Cree, which made him understand what the winds sometimes whispered in the pine-tops; and a part of him was French, which added jet to his eyes and a twist to his tongue and made him susceptible to the beautiful, and the rest was "just white" - the part of him that could be stirred into such thoughts and visions as he was now thinking and dreaming of the Englishman.

The "honor of the Beeg Snows" was a part of Jan's soul; it was his religion, and the religion of those few others who lived with him four hundred miles from a settlement, in a place where God's name could not be spelled or written. It meant what civilization could not understand, and the Englishman could not understand - freezing and slow starvation rather than theft, and the living of the tenth commandment above all other things. It came naturally and easily, this "honor of the Beeg Snows." It was an unwritten law which no man cared or dared to break, and to Jan, with his Cree and his French and his "just white" blood, it was in full measure just what the good God meant it to be.

He moved now toward the little isolated cabin, half hidden in its drift of snow, keeping well in the deep shadows of the spruce and balsam, and when he stopped again he saw faintly a gleam of light falling in a wan streak through a big hole in a curtained window. Each night, always when the twenty-odd souls of the post were deep in slumber, Jan's heart would come near to bursting with joy at the sight of this grow from the snow-smothered cabin, for it told him that the most beautiful thing in the world was safe and well. He heard, suddenly, the slamming of a door, and the young Englishman's whistle sounded shrill and untuneful as he went to his room in the factor's house. For a moment Jan straightened himself rigidly, and there was a strange tenseness in the thin, dark face that he turned straight up to where the Northern Lights were shivering in their midnight play. When he looked again at the light in the little cabin the passion-blood was rushing through his veins, and he fingered the hilt of the hunting knife in his belt.

The most beautiful thing in the world had come into Jan's life, and the other lives at the post, just two summers before. Cummins, red-headed, lithe as a cat, big-souled as the eternal mountain of the Crees and the best of the Company's hunters, had brought her up as his bride. Seventeen rough hearts had welcomed them. They had assembled about that little cabin in which the light was shining, speechless in their adoration of this woman who had come among them, their caps in their hands, faces shining, eyes shifting before the glorious ones that looked at them and smiled at them as the woman shook their hands, one by one. Perhaps she was not beautiful, as most people judge. But she was beautiful here - four hundred miles beyond civilization. Mukee, the half-Cree, had never seen a white woman, for even the factor's wife was part Chippewayan, and no one of the others went down to the edge of the southern wilderness more than once each twelve-month or so. Her hair was brown and soft, and it shone with a sunny glory that reached away back into their conception of things dreamed of but never seen, her eyes were as blue as the early snowflowers that came after the spring floods, and her voice was the sweetest sound that had ever fallen upon their ears. So these men thought when Cummins first brought home his wife, and the masterpiece which each had painted in his soul and brain was never changed. Each week and month added to the deep-toned value of that picture, as the passing of a century might add to a Raphael or a Van Dyke. The woman became more human, and less an angel, of course, but that only made her more real, and allowed them to become acquainted with her, to talk with her, and to love her more. There was no thought of wrong - until the Englishman came; for the devotion of these men who lived alone, and mostly wifeless, was a great passionless love unhinting of sin, and Cummins and his wife accepted it, and added to it when they could, and were the happiest pair in all that vast Northland.

The first year brought great changes. The girl - she was scarce more than budding into womanhood - fell happily into the ways of her new life. She did nothing that was elementally unusual - nothing more than any pure woman reared in the love of a God and home would have done. In her spare hours she began to teach the half dozen wild little children about the post, and every Sunday told them wonderful stories out of the Bible. She ministered to the sick, for that was a part of her code of life. Everywhere she carried her glad smile, her cheery greeting, her wistful earnestness to brighten what seemed to her the sad and lonely lives of these silent, worshipful men of the North. And she succeeded, not because she was unlike other millions of her kind, but because of the difference between the fortieth and the sixtieth degrees - the difference in the viewpoint of men who fought themselves into moral shreds in the big game of life and those who lived a thousand miles nearer to the dome of the earth. At the end of this first year came the wonderful event in the history of the Company's post, which had the Barren Lands at its back door. One day a new life was born into the little cabin of Cummins and his wife.

After this the silent, wordless worship of Jan and his people was filled with something very near to pathos. Cummins' wife was a mother. She was one of them now, a part of their indissoluble existence - a part of it as truly as the strange lights forever hovering over the Pole, as surely as the countless stars that never left the night skies, as surely as the endless forests and the deep snows! There was an added value to Cummins now. If there was a long and dangerous mission to perform it was somehow arranged so that he was left behind. Only Jan and one or two others knew why his traps made the best catch of fur, for more than once he had slipped a mink of an ermine or a fox into one of Cummins' traps, knowing that it would mean a luxury or two for the woman and the baby. And when Cummins left the post, sometimes for a day and sometimes longer, the mother and her child fell as a brief heritage to those who remained. The keenest eyes would not have discovered that this was so.

In the second year, with the beginning of trapping, fell the second and third great events. Cummins disappeared. Then came the Englishman. For a time the first of these two overshadowed everything else at the post. Cummins had gone to prospect a new trap-line, and was to sleep out the first night. The second night he was still gone. On the third day came the "Beeg Snow." It began at dawn, thickened as the day went, and continued to thicken until it became that soft, silent deluge of white in which no man dared venture a thousand yards from his door. The Aurora was hidden. There were no stars in the sky at night. Day was weighted with a strange, noiseless gloom. In all that wilderness there was not a creature that moved. Sixty hours later, when visible life was resumed again, the caribou, the wolf and the fox dug themselves up out of six feet of snow, and found the world changed.

It was at the beginning of the "Beeg Snow" that Jan went to the woman's cabin. He tapped upon her door with the timidity of a child, and when she opened it, her great eyes glowing at him in wild questioning, her face white with a terrible fear, there was a chill at his heart which choked back what he had come to say. He walked in dumbly and stood with the snow falling off him in piles, and when Cummins' wife saw neither hope nor foreboding in his dark, set face she buried her face in her arms upon the little table and sobbed softly in her despair. Jan strove to speak, but the Cree in him drove back what was French and "just white," and he stood in mute, trembling torture. "Ah, the Great God!" his soul was crying. "What can I do?"

Upon its little cot the woman's child was asleep. Beside the stove there were a few sticks of wood. He stretched himself until his neck creaked to see if there was water in the barrel near the door. Then he looked again at the bowed head and the shivering form at the table. In that moment Jan's resolution soared very near to the terrible.

"Mees Cummin, I go hunt for heem!" he cried. "I go hunt for heem - an' fin' heem!"

He waited another moment, and then backed softly toward the door.

"I hunt for heem!" he repeated, fearing that she had not heard.

She lifted her face, and the beating of Jan's heart sounded to him like the distant thrumming of partridge wings. Ah, the Great God - would he ever forget that look! She was coming to him, a new glory in her eyes, her arms reaching out, her lips parted! Jan knew how the Great Spirit had once appeared to Mukee, the half-Cree, and how a white mist, like a snow veil, had come between the half-breed's eyes and the wondrous thing he beheld. And that same snow veil drifted between Jan and the woman. Like in a vision he saw her glorious face so near to him that his blood was frightened into a strange, wonderful sensation that it had never known before. He felt the touch of her sweet breath, he heard her passionate prayer, he knew that one of his rough hands was clasped in both her own - and he knew, too, that their soft, thrilling warmth would remain with him until he died, and still go into Paradise with him.

When he trudged back into the snow, knee-deep now, he sought Mukee, the half-breed. Mukee had suffered a lynx bite that went deep into the bone, and Cummins' wife had saved his hand. After that the savage in him was enslaved to her like an invisible spirit, and when Jan slipped on his snowshoes to set out into the deadly chaos of the "Beeg Storm" Mukee was ready to follow. A trail through the spruce forest led them to the lake across which Jan knew that Cummins had intended to go. Beyond that, a matter of six miles or so, there was a deep and lonely break between two mountainous ridges in which Cummins believed he might find lynx. Indian instinct guided the two across the lake. There they separated, Jan going as nearly as he could guess into the northwest, Mukee trailing swiftly and hopelessly into the south, both inspired in the face of death by the thought of a woman with sunny hair, and with lips and eyes that had sent many a shaft of hope and gladness into their desolate hearts.

It was no great sacrifice for Jan, this struggle with the "Beeg Snows" for the woman's sake. What it was to Mukee, the half-Cree, no man ever guessed or knew, for it was not until the late spring snows had gone that they found what the foxes and the wolves had left of him, far to the south.

A hand, soft and gentle, guided Jan. He felt the warmth of it and the thrill of it, and neither the warmth nor the thrill grew less as the hours passed and the snow fell deeper. His soul was burning with a joy that it had never known. Beautiful visions danced in his brain, and always he heard the woman's voice praying to him in the little cabin, saw her eyes upon him through that white snow veil! Ah, what would he not give if he could find the man, if he could take Cummins back to his wife, and stand for one moment more with her hands clasping his, her joy flooding him with a sweetness that would last for all time! He plunged fearlessly into the white world beyond the lake, his wide snowshoes sinking ankle-deep at every step. There was neither rock nor tree to guide him, for everywhere was the heavy ghost-raiment of the Indian God. The balsams were bending under it, the spruces were breaking into hunchback forms, the whole world was twisted in noiseless torture under its increasing weight, and out through the still terror of it all Jan's voice went in wild echoing shouts. Now and then he fired his rifle, and always he listened long and intently. The echoes came back to him, laughing, taunting, and then each time fell the mirthless silence of the storm. Night came, a little darker than the day, and Jan stopped to build a fire and eat sparingly of his food, and to sleep. It was still night when he aroused himself and stumbled on. Never did he take the weight of his rifle from his right hand or shoulder, for he knew this weight would shorten the distance traveled at each step by his right foot, and would make him go in a circle that would bring him back to the lake. But it was a long circle. The day passed. A second night fell upon him, and his hope of finding Cummins was gone. A chill crept in where his heart had been so warm, and somehow that soft pressure of a woman's hand upon his seemed to become less and less real to him. The woman's prayers were following him, her heart was throbbing with its hope in him - and he had failed! On the third day, when the storm was over, Jan staggered hopelessly into the post. He went straight to the woman, disgraced, heartbroken. When he came out of the little cabin he seemed to have gone mad. A wondrously strange thing had happened. He had spoken not a word, but his failure and his sufferings were written in his face, and when Cummins' wife saw and understood she went as white as the underside of a poplar leaf in a clouded sun. But that was not all. She came to him, and clasped one of his half-frozen hands to her bosom, and he heard her say, "God bless you forever, Jan! You have done the best you could!" The Great God - was that not reward for the risking of a miserable, worthless life such as his? He went to his shack and slept long, and dreamed, sometimes of the woman, and of Cummins and Mukee, the half-Cree.

On the first crust of the new snow came the Englishman up from Fort Churchill, on Hudson's Bay. He came behind six dogs, and was driven by an Indian, and he bore letters to the factor which proclaimed him something of considerable importance at the home office of the Company, in London. As such he was given the best bed in the factor's rude home. On the second day he saw Cummins' wife at the Company's store, and very soon learned the history of Cummins' disappearance.

That was the beginning of the real tragedy at the post. The wilderness is a grim oppressor of life. To those who survive in it the going out of life is but an incident, an irresistible and natural thing, unpleasant but without horror. So it was with the passing of Cummins. But the Englishman brought with him something new, as the woman had brought something new, only in this instance it was an element of life which Jan and his people could not understand, an element which had never found a place, and never could, in the hearts and souls of the post. On the other hand, it promised to be but an incident to the Englishman, a passing adventure in pleasure common to the high and glorious civilization from which he had come. Here again was that difference of viewpoint, the eternity of difference between the middle and the end of the earth. As the days passed, and the crust grew deeper upon the "Beeg Snows," the tragedy progressed rapidly toward finality. At first Jan did not understand. The others did not understand. When the worm of the Englishman's sin revealed itself it struck them with a dumb, terrible fear.

The Englishman came from among women. For months he had been in a torment of desolation. Cummins' wife was to him like a flower suddenly come to relieve the tantalizing barrenness of a desert, and with the wiles and soft speech of his kind he sought to breathe its fragrance. In the weeks that followed the flower seemed to come nearer to him, and this was because Jan and his people had not as yet fully measured the heart of the woman, and because the Englishman had not measured Jan and his people he talked a great deal when enthused by the warmth of the box stove and his thoughts. So human passions were set at play. Because the woman knew nothing of what was said about the box stove she continued in the even course of her pure life, neither resisting nor encouraging the newcomer, yet ever tempting him with that sweetness which she gave to all alike, and still praying in the still hours of night that Cummins would return to her. As yet there was no suspicion in her soul. She accepted the Englishman's friendship. His sympathy for her won him a place in her recognition of things good and true. She did not hear the false note, she saw no step that promised evil. Only Jan and his people saw and understood the one-sided struggle, and shivered at the monstrous evil of it. At least they thought they saw and understood, which was enough. Like so many faithful beasts they were ready to spring, to rend flesh, to tear life out of him who threatened the desecration of all that was good and pure and beautiful to them, and yet, dumb in their devotion and faith, they waited and watched for a sign from the woman. The blue eyes of Cummins' wife, the words of her gentle lips, the touch of her hands had made law at the post. She, herself, had become the omniscience of all that was law to them, and if she smiled upon the Englishman, and talked with him, and was pleased with him, that was only one other law that she had made for them to respect. So they were quiet, evaded the Englishman as much as possible, and watched - always watch ed.

These were days when something worse than disease was eating at the few big honest hearts that made up the life at the post. The search for Cummins never ceased, and always the woman was receiving hope. Now it was Williams who went far into the South, and brought back word that a strange white man had been seen among the Indians; then it was Thoreau, the Frenchman, who skirted the edge of the Barren Lands three days into the West, and said that he had found the signs of strange campfires. And always Jan was on the move, to the South, the North, the East and the West. The days began to lengthen. It was dawn now at eight o'clock instead of nine, the silvery white of the sun was turning day by day more into the glow of fire, and for a few minutes at midday the snow softened and water dripped from the roofs.

Jan knew what it meant. Very soon the thick crust of the "Beeg Snow" would drop in, and they would find Cummins. They would bring what was left of him back to the post. And then - what would happen then?

Every day or two Jan found some pretext that took him to the little log cabin. Now it was to convey to the woman a haunch of a caribou he had slain. Again it was to bring her child a strange plaything from the forest. More frequently it was to do the work that Cummins would have done. He seldom went within the low door, but stood outside, speaking a few words, while Cummins' wife talked to him. But one morning, when the sun was shining down with the first promising warmth of spring, the woman stepped hack from the door and asked him in.

"I want to tell you something, Jan," she said softly. "I have been thinking about it for a long time. I must find some work to do. I must do something - to earn - money."

Jan's eyes leaped straight to hers in sudden horror.

"Work!"

The word fell from him as if in its utterance there was something of crime. Then he stood speechless, awed by the look in her eyes, the hard gray pallor that came into her face.

"May God bless you for all you have done, Jan, and may God bless the others! I want you to take that word to them from me. But he will never come back, Jan - never. Tell the men that I love them as brothers, and always shall love them, but now that I know he is dead I can no longer live as a drone among them. I will do anything. I will make your coats, do your washing and mend your moccasins. To-morrow I begin my first work - for money."

He heard what she said after that as if in a dream. When he went out into the day again, with her word to his people, he knew that in some way which he could not understand this big, cold world had changed for him. To-morrow Cummins' wife was to begin writing letters for the Englishman! His eyes glittered, his hands clenched themselves upon his breast, and all the blood in him submerged itself in one wild resistless impulse. An hour later Jan and his four dogs were speeding swiftly into the South.

The next day the Englishman went to the woman's cabin. He did not return in the afternoon. And that same afternoon, when Cummins' wife came into the Company's store, a quick flush shot into her cheeks and the glitter of blue diamonds into her eyes when she saw the Englishman standing there. The man's red face grew redder, and he shifted his gaze. When Cummins' wife passed him she drew her skirt close to her, and there was the poise of a queen in her head, the glory of mother and wife and womanhood, the living, breathing essence of all that was beautiful in Jan's "honor of the Beeg Snows." But Jan, twenty miles to the south, did not know.

He returned on the fourth night and went quietly to his little shack in the edge of the balsam forest. In the glow of the oil lamp which he lighted he rolled up his treasure of winter-caught furs into a small pack. Then he opened his door and walked straight and fearlessly toward the cabin of Cummins' wife. It was a pale, glorious night, and Jan lifted his face to its starry skies and filled his lungs near to bursting with its pure air, and when he was within a few steps of the woman's door he burst into a wild snatch of triumphant forest song. For this was a new Jan who was returning to her, a man who had gone out into the solitudes and fought a great battle with the elementary things in him, and who, because of his triumph over these things, was filled with the strength and courage to live a great lie. The woman heard his voice, and recognized it. The door swung open, wide and brimful of light, and in it stood Cummins' wife, her child hugged close in her arms.

James Oliver Curwood

Jan crowed close up out of the starry gloom.

"I fin' heem, Mees Cummins - I fin' heem nint' miles back in Cree wigwam - with broke leg. He come home soon - he sen' great love - an' THESE!"

And he dropped his furs at the woman's feet....

"Ah, the Great God!" cried Jan's tortured soul when it was all over. "At least she shall not work for the dirty Englishman."

First he awoke the factor, and told him what he had done. Then he went to Williams, and after that, one by one, these three visited the four other white and part white men at the post. They lived very near to the earth, these seven, and the spirit of the golden rule was as natural to their living as green sap to the trees. So they stood shoulder to shoulder to Jan in a scheme that appalled them, and in the very first day of this scheme they saw the woman blossoming forth in her old beauty and joy, and at times fleeting visions of the old happiness at the post came to these lonely men who were searing their souls for her. But to Jan one vision came to destroy all others, and as the old light returned to the woman's eyes, the glad smile to her lips, the sweetness of thankfulness and faith into her voice, this vision hurt him until he rolled and tossed in agony at night, and by day his feet were never still. His search for Cummins now had something of madness in it. It was his one hope - where to the other six there was no hope. And one day this spark went out of him. The crust was gone. The snow was settling. Beyond the lake he found the chasm between the two mountains, and, miles of this chasm, robbed to the bones of flesh, he found Cummins. The bones , and Cummins' gun, and all that was left of him, he buried in a crevasse.

He waited until night to return to the post. Only one light was burning when he came out into the clearing, and that was the light in the woman's cabin. In the edge of the balsams he sat down to watch it, as he had watched it a hundred nights before. Suddenly something came between him and the light. Against the cabin he saw the shadow of a human form, and as silently as the steely flash of the Aurora over his head, as swiftly as a lean deer, he sped through the gloom of the forest's edge and came up behind the home of the woman and her child. With the caution of a lynx, his head close to the snow, he peered around the end of the logs. It was the Englishman who stood looking through the tear in the curtained window! Jan's moccasined feet made no sound. His hand fell as gently as a child's upon the Englishman's arm.

"Thees is not the honor of the Beeg Snows!" he whispered. "Come."

A sickly pallor filled the Englishman's face. But Jan's voice was soft and dispassionate, his touch was velvety in its hint, and he went with the guiding hand away from the curtained window, smiling in a companionable way. Jan's teeth gleamed back. The Englishman chuckled. Then Jan's hands changed. They flew to the thick reddening throat of the man from civilization, and without a sound the two sank together upon the snow. It was many minutes before Jan rose to his feet. The next day Williams set out for Fort Churchill with word for the Company's home office that the Englishman had died in the "Beeg Snow," which was true.

The end was not far away now. Jan was expecting it day by day, hour by hour. But it came in a way that he did not expect. A month had gone, and Cummins had not come up from among the Crees. At times there was a strange light in the woman's eyes as she questioned the men at the post. Then, one day, the factor's son told Jan that she wanted to see him in the little cabin at the other end of the clearing.

A shiver went through him as he came to the door. It was more than a spirit of unrest in Jan to-day, more than suspicion, more than his old dread of that final moment of the tragedy he was playing, which would condemn him to everlasting perdition in the woman's eyes. It was pain, poignant, terrible - something which he could not name, something upon which he could place his hand, and yet which filled him with a desire to throw himself upon his face in the snow and sob out his grief as he had seen the little children do. It was not dread, but the torment of reality, that gripped him now, and when he faced the woman he knew why. There had come a terrible change, but a quiet change, in Cummins' wife. The luster had gone from her eyes. There was a dead whiteness in her face that went to the roots of her shimmering hair, and as she spoke to Jan she clutched one hand upon her bosom, which rose and fell as Jan had seen the breast of a mother lynx rise and fall in the last torture of its death.

"Jan," she panted, "Jan - you have lied to me!"

Jan's head dropped. The worn caribou skin of his coat crumpled upon his breast. His heart died. And yet he found voice, soft, low, simple.

"Yes, me lie!"

"You - you lied to me!"

"Yes - me - lie - "

His head dropped lower. He heard the sobbing breath of the woman, and gently his arm crooked itself, and his fingers rose slowly, very slowly, toward the hilt of his hunting knife.

"Yes - Mees Cummins - me lie - "

There came a sudden swift, sobbing movement, and the woman was at Jan's feet, clasping his hand to her bosom as she had clasped it once before when he had gone out to face death for her. But this time the snow veil was very thick before Jan's eyes, and he did not see her face. Only he heard.

"Bless you, dear Jan, and may God bless you evermore! For you have been good to me, Jan - so good - to me - "

And he went out into the day again a few moments later, leaving her alone in her great grief, for Jan was a man in the wild and mannerless ways of a savage world, and he knew not how to comfort in the fashion of that other world which had other conceptions and another understanding of what was to him the "honor of the Beeg Snows." A week later the woman announced her intention of returning to her people, for the dome of the earth had grown sad and lonely and desolate to her now that Cummins was forever gone. Sometimes the death of a beloved friend brings with it the sadness that spread like a pall over Jan and those others who had lived very near to contentment and happiness for nearly two years, only each knew that

182   James Oliver Curwood

this grief of his would be as enduring as life itself. For a brief space the sweetest of all God's things had come among them, a pure woman who brought with her the gentleness and beauty and hallowed thoughts of civilization in place of its iniquities, and the pictures in their hearts were imperishable.

The parting was as simple and as quiet as when the woman had come. They went to the little cabin where the sledge dogs stood harnessed. Hatless, silent, crowding back their grief behind grim and lonely countenances, they waited for Cummins' wife to say good-bye. The woman did not speak. She held up her child for each man to kiss, and the baby babbled meaningless things into the bearded faces that it had come to know and love, and when it came to Williams' turn he whispered, "Be a good baby, be a good baby." And when it was all over the woman crushed the child to her breast and dropped sobbing upon the sledge, and Jan cracked his whip and shouted hoarsely to the dogs, for it was Jan who was to drive her to civilization. Long after they had disappeared beyond the clearing those who remained stood looking at the cabin; and then, with a dry, strange sob in his throat, Williams led the way inside. When they came out Williams brought a hammer with him, and nailed the door tight.

"Mebby she'll come back some day," he said.

That was all, but the others understood.

For nine days Jan raced his dogs into the South. On the tenth they came to Le Pas. It was night when they stopped before the little log hotel, and the gloom hid the twitching in Jan's face.

"You will stay here - to-night?" asked the woman.

"Me go back - now," said Jan.

Cummins' wife came very close to him. She did not urge, for she, too, was suffering the torture of this last parting with the "honor of the Beeg Snows." It was not the baby's face that came to Jan's now, but the woman's. He felt the soft touch of her lips, and his soul burst forth in a low, agonized cry.

"The good God bless you, and keep you, and care for you evermore, Jan," she whispered. "Some day we will meet again."

And she kissed him again, and lifted the child to him, and Jan turned his tired dogs back into the grim desolation of the North, where the Aurora was lighting his way feebly, and beckoning to him, and telling him that the old life of centuries and centuries ago was waiting for him there.

BUCKY SEVERN

Father Brochet had come south from Fond du Lac, and Weyman, the Hudson's Bay Company doctor, north through the Geikee River country. They had met at Severn's cabin, on the Waterfound. Both had come on the same mission - to see Severn; one to keep him from dying, if that was possible, one to comfort him in the last hour, if death came. Severn insisted on living. Bright-eyed, hollow-cheeked, with a racking cough that reddened the gauze handkerchief the doctor had given him, he sat bolstered up in his cot and looked out through the open door with glad and hopeful gaze. Weyman had arrived only half an hour before. Outside was the Indian canoeman who had helped to bring him up.

It was a glorious day, such as comes in its full beauty only in the far northern spring, where the air enters the lungs like sharp, warm wine, laden with the tang of spruce and balsam, and the sweetness of the bursting poplar-buds.

"It was mighty good of you to come up," Severn was saying to the doctor. "The company has always been the best friend I've ever had - except one - and that's why I've hung to it all these years, trailing the sledges first as a kid, you know, then trapping, running, and - oh, Lord!"

He stopped to cough, and the little black-frocked missioner, looking across at Weyman, saw him bite his lips.

"That cough hurts, but it's better," Severn apologized, smiling weakly. "Funny, ain't it, a man like me coming down with a cough? Why, I've slept in ice a thousand times, with snow for a pillow and the thermometer down to fifty. But this last winter it was cold, seventy or lower, an' I worked in it when I ought to have been inside, warming my toes. But, you see, I wanted to get the cabin built, an' things all cleared up about here, before SHE came. It's the cold that got me, wasn't it, doc?"

"That's it," said Weyman, rolling and lighting a cigarette. Then he laughed, as the sick man finished another coughing spell, and said:

"I never thought you'd have a love affair, Bucky!"

"Neither did I," chuckled Severn. "Ain't it a wonder, doc? Here I'm thirty-eight, with a hide on me like leather, an' no thought of a woman for twenty years, until I saw HER. I don't mean it's a wonder I fell in love, doc - you'd 'a' done that if you'd met her first. The wonder of it is that she fell in love with me." He laughed softly. "I'll bet Father Brochet'll go in a heap himself when he marries us! It's goin' to happen next month. Did you ever see her, father - Marie La Corne, over at the post on Split Lake?"

Severn dropped his head to cough, but Weyman say the sudden look of horror that leaped into the little priest's face.

"Marie La Corne!"

"Yes, at Split Lake."

Severn looked up again. He had missed what Weyman had seen.

"Yes, I've seen her."

Bucky Severn's eyes lit up with pleasure.

"She's - she's beautiful, ain't she?" he cried in hoarse whisper. "Ain't it a wonder, father? I come up there with a canoe full of supplies, last spring about this time, an' - an' at first I hardly dast to look at her; but it came out all right. When I told her I was coming over here to build us a home, she wanted me to bring her along to help; but I wouldn't. I knew it was goin' to be hard this winter, and she's never goin' to work - never so long as I live. I ain't had much to do with women, but I've seen 'em and I've watched 'em an' she's never goin' to drudge like the rest. If she'll let me, I'm even goin' to do the cookin' an' the dish-washing and scrub the floors! I've done it for twenty-five years, an' I'm tough. She ain't goin' to do nothin' but sew for the kids when they come, an' sing, an' be happy. When it comes to the work that there ain't no fun in, I'll do it. I've planned it all out. We're goin' to have half an arpent square of flowers, an' she'll love to work among 'em. I've got the ground cleared - out there - you kin see it by twisting your head through the door. An' she's goin' to have an organ. I've got the money saved, an' it's coming to Churchill on the next ship. That's goin' to be a surprise - 'bout Christmas, when the snow is hard an' sledging good. You see - "

He stopped again to cough. A hectic flush filled his hollow cheeks, and there was a feverish glow in his eyes. As he bent his head, the priest looked at Weyman. The doctor's lips were tense. His cigarette was unlighted.

"I know what it means for a woman to die a workin'," Severn went on. "My mother did that. I can remember it, though I was only a kid. She was bent an' stoop-shouldered, an' her hands were rough and twisted. I know now why she used to hug me up close and croon funny things over me when father was away. When I first told my Marie what I was goin' to do, she laughed at me; but when I told her 'bout my mother, an' how work an' freezin' an' starvin' killed her when I needed her most, Marie jest put her hand up to my face an' looked queer - an' then she burst out crying like a baby. She understands, Marie does! She knows what I'm goin' to do - "

"You mustn't talk any more, Bucky," warned the doctor, feeling his pulse. "It'll hurt you."

"Hurt me!" Severn laughed hysterically, as If what the doctor had said was a joke. "Hurt me? It's what's going to put me on my feet, doc. I know it now, I been too much alone this last winter, with nothin' but my dogs to talk to when night come. I ain't never been much of a talker, but she got me out o' that. She used to tease me at first, an' I'd get red in the face an' almost bust. An' then, one day, it come, like a bung out of a hole, an' I've had a hankerin' to talk ever since. Hurt me!"

He gave an incredulous chuckle, which ended in a cough.

"Do you know, I wish I could read better 'n I can!" he said suddenly, leaning almost eagerly toward Father Brochet. "She knows I ain't great shucks at that. She's goin' to have a school just as soon as she comes, an' I'm goin' to be the scholar. She's got a packful of books an' magazines an' I'm goin' to tote over a fresh load every winter. I'd like to surprise her. Can't you help me to - "

Weyman pressed him back gently.

"See here, Bucky, you've got to lie down and keep quiet," he said. "If you don't, it will take you a week longer to get well. Try and sleep a little, while Father Brochet and I go outside and see what you've done."

When they went out, Weyman closed the door after them. He spoke no word as he turned and looked upon what Bucky Severn had done for the coming of his bride. Father Brochet's hand touched the doctor's and it was cold and trembling.

"How is he?" he asked.

"It is the bad malady," said Weyman softly. "The frost has touched his lungs. One does not feel the effect of that until spring comes. Then - a cough - and the lungs begin literally to slough away."

"You mean - "

"That there is no hope - absolutely none. He will die within two days."

As he spoke, the little priest straightened himself and lifted his hands as if about to pronounce a benediction.

"Thank God!" he breathed. Then, as quickly, he caught himself. "No, I don't mean that. God forgive me! But - it is best." Weyman stared incredulously into his face.

"It is best," repeated the other, as gently as if speaking a prayer. "How strangely the Creator sometimes works out His ends! I came straight here from Split Lake. Marie La Corne died two weeks ago. It was I who said the last prayer over her dead body!"

HIS FIRST PENITENT

In a white wilderness of moaning storm, in a wilderness of miles and miles of black pine-trees, the Transcontinental Flier lay buried in the snow. In the first darkness of the wild December night, engine and tender had rushed on ahead to division headquarters, to let the line know that the flier had given up the fight, and needed assistance. They had been gone two hours, and whiter and whiter grew the brilliantly lighted coaches in the drifts and winnows of the whistling storm. From the black edges of the forest, prowling eyes might have looked upon scores of human faces staring anxiously out into the blackness from the windows of the coaches.

In those coaches it was growing steadily colder. Men were putting on their overcoats, and women snuggled deeper in their furs. Over it all, the tops of the black pine-trees moaned and whistled in sounds that seemed filled both with menace and with savage laughter.

In the smoking-compartment of the Pullman sat five men, gathered in a group. Of these, one was Forsythe, the timber agent; two were traveling men; the fourth a passenger homeward bound from a holiday visit; and the fifth was Father Charles. The priest's pale, serious face lit up in surprise or laughter with the others, but his lips had not broken into a story of their own. He was a little man, dressed in somber black, and there was that about him which told his companions that within his tight-drawn coat of shiny black there were hidden tales which would have gone well with the savage beat of the storm against the lighted windows and the moaning tumult of the pine-trees.

Suddenly Forsythe shivered at a fiercer blast than the others, and said:

"Father, have you a text that would fit this night - and the situation?"

Slowly Father Charles blew out a spiral of smoke from between his lips, and then he drew himself erect and leaned a little forward, with the cigar between his slender white fingers.

"I had a text for this night," he said, "but I have none now, gentlemen. I was to have married a couple a hundred miles down the line. The guests have assembled. They are ready, but I am not there. The wedding will not be to-night, and so my text is gone. But there comes another to my mind which fits this situation - and a thousand others - 'He who sits in the heavens shall look down and decide.' To-night I was to have married these young people. Three hours ago I never dreamed of doubting that I should be on hand at the appointed hour. But I shall not marry them. Fate has enjoined a hand. The Supreme Arbiter says 'No,' and what may not be the consequences'?"

"They will probably be married to-morrow," said one of the traveling men. " There will be a few hours' delay - nothing more."

"Perhaps," replied Father Charles, as quietly as before. "And - perhaps not. Who can say what this little incident may not mean in the lives of that young man and that young woman - and, it may be, in my own? Three or four hours lost in a storm - what may they not mean to more than one human heart on this train? The Supreme Arbiter plays His hand, if you wish to call it that, with reason and intent. To someone, somewhere, the most insignificant occurrence may mean life or death. And to-night - this - means something."

A sudden blast drove the night screeching over our heads, and the whining of the pines was almost like human voices. Forsythe sucked a cigar that had gone out.

"Long ago," said Father Charles, "I knew a young man and a young woman who were to be married. The man went West to win a fortune. Thus fate separated them, and in the lapse of a year such terrible misfortune came to the girl's parents that she was forced into a marriage with wealth - a barter of her white body for an old man's gold. When the young man returned from the West he found his sweetheart married, and hell upon earth was their lot. But hope lingers in your hearts. He waited four years; and then, discouraged, he married another woman. Gentlemen, three days after the wedding his old sweetheart's husband died, and she was released from bondage. Was not that the hand of the Supreme Arbiter? If he had waited but three days more, the old happiness might have lived.

"But wait! One month after that day the young man was arrested, taken to a Western State, tried for murder, and hanged. Do you see the point? In three days more the girl who had sold herself into slavery for the salvation of those she loved would have been released from her bondage only to marry a murderer!"

There was silence, in which all five listened to that wild moaning of the storm. There seemed to be something in it now - something more than the inarticulate sound of wind and trees. Forsythe scratched a match and relighted his cigar.

"I never thought of such things in just that light," he said.

"Listen to the wind," said the little priest. "Hear the pine-trees shriek out there! It recalls to me a night of years and years ago - a night like this, when the storm moaned and twisted about my little cabin, and when the Supreme Arbiter sent me my first penitent. Gentlemen, it is something which will bring you nearer to an understanding of the voice and the hand of God. It is a sermon on the mighty significance of little things, this story of my first penitent. If you wish, I will tell it to you."

"Go on," said Forsythe.

The traveling men drew nearer.

"It was a night like this," repeated Father Charles, "and it was in a great wilderness like this, only miles and miles away. I had been sent to establish a mission; and in my cabin, that wild night, alone and with the storm shrieking about me, I was busy at work sketching out my plans. After a time I grew nervous. I did not smoke then, and so I had nothing to comfort me but my thoughts; and, in spite of my efforts to make them otherwise, they were cheerless enough. The forest grew to my door. In the fiercer blasts I could hear the lashing of the pine-trees over my head, and now and then an arm of one of the moaning trees would reach down and sweep across my cabin roof with a sound that made me shudder and fear. This wilderness fear is an oppressive and terrible thing when you are alone at night, and the world is twisting and tearing itself outside. I have heard the pine-trees shriek like dying women, I have heard them wailing like lost children, I have heard them sobbing and moaning like human souls writhing in agony - "

Father Charles paused, to peer through the window out into the black night, where the pine-trees were sobbing and moaning now. When he turned, Forsythe, the timber agent, whose life was a wilderness life, nodded understandingly.

"And when they cry like that," went on Father Charles, "a living voice would be lost among them as the splash of a pebble is lost in the roaring sea. A hundred times that night I fancied that I heard human voices; and a dozen times I went to my door, drew back the bolt, and listened, "with the snow and the wind beating about my ears.

"As I sat shuddering before my fire, there came a thought to me of a story which I had long ago read about the sea - a story of impossible achievement and of impossible heroism. As vividly as if I had read it only the day before, I recalled the description of a wild and stormy night when the heroine placed a lighted lamp in the window of her sea-bound cottage, to guide her lover home in safety. Gentlemen, the reading of that book in my boyhood days was but a trivial thing. I had read a thousand others, and of them all it was possibly the least significant; but the Supreme Arbiter had not forgotten.

"The memory of that book brought me to my feet, and I placed a lighted lamp close up against my cabin window. Fifteen minutes later I heard a strange sound at the door, and when I opened it there fell in upon the floor at my feet a young and beautiful woman. And after her, dragging himself over the threshold on his hands and knees, there came a man.

"I closed the door, after the man had crawled in and fallen face downward upon the floor, and turned my attention first to the woman. She was covered with snow. Her long, beautiful hair was loose and disheveled, and had blown about her like a veil. Her big, dark eyes looked at me pleadingly, and in them there was a terror such as I had never beheld in human eyes before. I bent over her, intending to carry her to my cot; but in another moment she had thrown herself upon the prostrate form of the man, with her arms about his head, and there burst from her lips the first sounds that she had uttered. They were not much more intelligible than the wailing grief of the pine-trees out in the night, but they told me plainly enough that the man on the floor was dearer to her than life.

"I knelt beside him, and found that he was breathing in a quick, panting sort of way, and that his wide-open eyes were looking at the woman. Then I noticed for the first time that his face was cut and bruised, and his lips were swollen. His coat was loose at the throat, and I could see livid marks on his neck.

"'I'm all right,' he whispered, struggling for breath, and turning his eyes to me. 'We should have died - in a few

James Oliver Curwood

minutes more - if it hadn't been for the light in your window!'

"The young woman bent down and kissed him, and then she allowed me to help her to my cot. When I had attended to the young man, and he had regained strength enough to stand upon his feet, she was asleep. The man went to her, and dropped upon his knees beside the cot. Tenderly he drew back the heavy masses of hair from about her face and shoulders. For several minutes he remained with his face pressed close against hers; then he rose, and faced me. The woman - his wife - knew nothing of what passed between us during the next half-hour. During that half-hour gentlemen, I received my first confession. The young man was of my faith. He was my first penitent."

It was growing colder in the coach, and Father Charles stopped to draw his thin black coat closer to him. Forsythe relighted his cigar for the third time. The transient passenger gave a sudden start as a gust of wind beat against the window like a threatening hand.

"A rough stool was my confessional, gentlemen," resumed Father Charles. "He told me the story, kneeling at my feet - a story that will live with me as long as I live, always reminding me that the little things of life may be the greatest things, that by sending a storm to hold up a coach the Supreme Arbiter may change the map of the world. It is not a long story. It is not even an unusual story.

"He had come into the North about a year before, and had built for himself and his wife a little home at a pleasant river spot ten miles distant from my cabin. Their love was of the kind we do not often see, and they were as happy as the birds that lived about them in the wilderness. They had taken a timber claim. A few months more, and a new life was to come into their little home; and the knowledge of this made the girl an angel of beauty and joy. Their nearest neighbor was another man, several miles distant. The two men became friends, and the other came over to see them frequently. It was the old, old story. The neighbor fell in love with the young settler's wife.

"As you shall see, this other man was a beast. On the day preceding the night of the terrible storm, the woman's husband set out for the settlement to bring back supplies. Hardly had he gone, when the beast came to the cabin. He found himself alone with the woman.

"A mile from his cabin, the husband stopped to light his pipe. See, gentlemen, how the Supreme Arbiter played His hand. The man attempted to unscrew the stem, and the stem broke. In the wilderness you must smoke. Smoke is your company. It is voice and companionship to you. There were other pipes at the settlement, ten miles away; but there was also another pipe at the cabin, one mile away. So the husband turned back. He came up quietly to his door, thinking that he would surprise his wife. He heard voices - a man's voice, a woman's cries. He opened the door, and in the excitement of what was happening within neither the man nor the woman saw nor heard him. They were struggling. The woman was in the man's arms, her hair torn down, her small hands beating him in the face, her breath coming in low, terrified cries. Even as the husband stood there for the fraction of a second, taking in the terrible scene, the other man caught the woman's face to him, and kissed her. And then - it happened.

"It was a terrible fight; and when it was over the beast lay on the floor, bleeding and dead. Gentlemen, the Supreme Arbiter BROKE A PIPE-STEM, and sent the husband back in time!"

No one spoke as Father Charles drew his coat still closer about him. Above the tumult of the storm another sound came to them - the distant, piercing shriek of a whistle.

"The husband dug a grave through the snow and in the frozen earth," concluded Father Charles; "and late that afternoon they packed up a bundle and set out together for the settlement. The storm overtook them. They had dropped for the last time into the snow, about to die in each other's arms, when I put my light in the window. That is all; except that I knew them for several years afterward, and that the old happiness returned to them - and more, for the child was born, a miniature of its mother. Then they moved to another part of the wilderness, and I to still another. So you see, gentlemen, what a snow-bound train may mean, for if an old sea tale, a broken pipe-stem - "

The door at the end of the smoking-room opened suddenly. Through it there came a cold blast of the storm, a cloud of snow, and a man. He was bundled in a great bearskin coat, and as he shook out its folds his strong, ruddy face smiled cheerfully at those whom he had interrupted.

Then, suddenly, there came a change in his face. The merriment went from it. He stared at Father Charles. The priest was rising, his face more tense and whiter still, his hands reaching out to the stranger.

In another moment the stranger had leaped to him - not to shake his hands, but to clasp the priest in his great arms, shaking him, and crying out a strange joy, while for the first time that night the pale face of Father Charles was lighted up with a red and joyous glow.

After several minutes the newcomer released Father Charles, and turned to the others with a great hearty laugh.

"Gentlemen," he said, "you must pardon me for interrupting you like this. You will understand when I tell you that Father Charles is an old friend of mine, the dearest friend I have on earth, and that I haven't seen him for years. I was his first penitent!"

PETER GOD

Peter God was a trapper. He set his deadfalls and fox-baits along the edge of that long, slim finger of the Great Barren, which reaches out of the East well into the country of the Great Bear, far to the West. The door of his sapling-built cabin opened to the dark and chilling gray of the Arctic Circle; through its one window he could watch the sputter and play of the Northern Lights; and the curious hissing purr of the Aurora had grown to be a monotone in his ears.

Whence Peter God had come, and how it was that he bore the strange name by which he went, no man had asked, for curiosity belongs to the white man, and the nearest white men were up at Fort MacPherson, a hundred or so miles away.

Six or seven years ago Peter God had come to the post for the first time with his furs. He had given his name as Peter God, and the Company had not questioned it, or wondered. Stranger names than Peter's were a part of the Northland; stranger faces than his came in out of the white wilderness trails; but none was more silent, or came in and went more quickly. In the gray of the afternoon he drove in with his dogs and his furs; night would see him on his way back to the Barrens, supplies for another three months of loneliness on his sledge.

It would have been hard to judge his age - had one taken the trouble to try. Perhaps he was thirty-eight. He surely was not French. There was no Indian blood in him. His heavy beard was reddish, his long thick hair distinctly blond, and his eyes were a bluish-gray.

For seven years, season after season, the Hudson's Bay Company's clerk had written items something like the following in his record-books:

Feb. 17. Peter God came in to-day with his furs. He leaves this afternoon or to-night for his trapping grounds with fresh supplies.

The year before, in a momentary fit of curiosity, the clerk had added:

Curious why Peter God never stays in Fort MacPherson overnight.

And more curious than this was the fact that Peter God never asked for mail, and no letter ever came to Fort MacPherson for him.

The Great Barren enveloped him and his mystery. The yapping foxes knew more of him than men. They knew him for a hundred miles up and down that white finger of desolation; they knew the peril of his baits and his deadfalls; they snarled and barked their hatred and defiance at the glow of his lights on dark nights; they watched for him, sniffed for signs of him, and walked into his clever deathpits.

The foxes and Peter God! That was what this white world was made up of - foxes and Peter God. It was a world of strife between them. Peter God was killing - but the foxes were winning. Slowly but surely they were breaking him down - they and the terrible loneliness. Loneliness Peter God might have stood for many more years. But the foxes were driving him mad. More and more he had come to dread their yapping at night. That was the deadly combination - night and the yapping. In the day-time he laughed at himself for his fears; nights he sweated, and sometimes wanted to scream. What manner of man Peter God was or might have been, and of the strangeness of the life that was lived in the maddening loneliness of that mystery-cabin in the edge of the Barren, only one other man knew.

That was Philip Curtis.

Two thousand miles south, Philip Curtis sat at a small table in a brilliantly lighted and fashionable cafe. It was early June, and Philip had been down from the North scarcely a month, the deep tan was still in his face, and tiny wind and snow lines crinkled at the corners of his eyes. He exuded the life of the big outdoors as he sat opposite pallid-cheeked and weak-chested Barrow, the Mica King, who would have given his millions to possess the red blood in the other's veins.

Philip had made his "strike," away up on the Mackenzie. That day he had sold out to Barrow for a hundred thousand. To-night he was filled with the flush of joy and triumph.

Barrow's eyes shone with a new sort of enthusiasm as he listened to this man's story of grim and fighting determination that had led to the discovery of that mountain of mica away up on the Clearwater Bulge.

He looked upon the other's strength, his bronzed face and the glory of achievement in his eyes, and a great and yearning hopelessness burned like a dull fire in his heart. He was no older than the man who sat on the other side of the table - perhaps thirty-five; yet what a vast gulf lay between them! He with his millions; the other with that flood of red blood coming and going in his body, and his wonderful fortune of a hundred thousand! Barrow leaned a little over the table, and laughed. It was the laugh of a man who had grown tired of life, in spite of his millions. Day before yesterday a famous specialist had warned him that the threads of his life were giving way, one by one. He told this to Curtis. He confessed to him, with that strange glow in his eyes, - a glow that was like making a last fight against total extinguishment, - that he would give up his millions and all he had won for the other's health and the mountain of mica.

"And if it came to a close bargain," he said, "I wouldn't hold out for the mountain. I'm ready to quit - and it's too late."

Which, after a little, brought Philip Curtis to tell so much as he knew of the story of Peter God. Philip's voice was tuned with the winds and the forests. It rose above the low and monotonous hum about them. People at the two or three adjoining tables might have heard his story, if they had listened. Within the immaculateness of his evening dress, Barrows shivered, fearing that Curtis' voice might attract undue attention to them. But other people were absorbed in themselves. Philip went on with his story, and at last, so clearly that it reached easily to the other tables, he spoke the name of Peter God.

Then came the interruption, and with that interruption a strange and sudden upheaval in the life of Philip Curtis that was to mean more to him than the discovery of the mica mountain. His eyes swept over Barrow's shoulder, and there he saw a woman. She was standing. A low, stifled cry had broken from her almost simultaneously with his first glimpse of her, and as he looked, Philip saw her lips form gaspingly the name he had spoken - Peter God!

She was so near that Barrow could have turned and touched her. Her eyes were like luminous fires as she stared at Philip. Her face was strangely pale. He could see her quiver, and catch her breath. And she was looking at him. For that one moment she had forgotten the presence of others.

Then a hand touched her arm. It was the hand of her elderly escort, in whose face were anxiety and wonder. The woman started and took her eyes from Philip. With her escort she seated herself at a table a few paces away, and for a few moments Philip could see she was fighting for composure, and that it cost her a struggle to keep her eyes from turning in his direction while she talked in a low voice to her companion.

Philip's heart was pounding like an engine. He knew that she was talking about him now, and he knew that she had cried out when he had spoken Peter God's name. He forgot Barrow as he looked at her. She was exquisite, even with that gray pallor that had come so suddenly into her cheeks. She was not young, as the age of youth is measured. Perhaps she was thirty, or thirty-two, or thirty-five. If some one had asked Philip to describe her, he would have said simply that she was glorious. Yet her entrance had caused no stir. Few had looked at her until she had uttered that sharp cry. There were a score of women under the brilliantly lighted chandeliers possessed of more spectacular beauty, Barrow had partly turned in his seat, and now, with careful breeding, he faced his companion again.

"Do you know her?" Philip asked.

Barrow shook his head.

"No." Then he added: "Did you see what made her cry out like that?"

"I believe so," said Philip, and he turned purposely so that the four people at the next table could hear him. "I think she twisted her ankle. It's an occasional penance the women make for wearing these high-heeled shoes, you know."

He looked at her again. Her form was bent toward the white-haired man who was with her. The man was staring straight over at Philip, a strange searching look in his face as he listened to what she was saying. He seemed to question Philip through the short distance that separated them. And then the woman turned her head slowly, and once more Philip met her eyes squarely - deep, dark, glowing eyes that thrilled him to the quick of his soul. He did not try to understand what he saw in them. Before he turned his glance to Barrow he saw that color had swept back into her face; her lips were parted; he knew that she was struggling to suppress a tremendous emotion.

Barrow was looking at him curiously - and Philip went on with his story of Peter God. He told it in a lower voice. Not until he had finished did he look again in the direction of the other table. The woman had changed her position slightly, so that he could not see her face. The uptilt of her hat revealed to him the warm soft glow of shining coils of brown hair. He was sure that her escort was keeping watch of his movements.

Suddenly Barrow drew his attention to a man sitting alone a dozen tables from them.

"There's DeVoe, one of the Amalgamated chiefs," he said. "He has almost finished, and I want to speak to him before he leaves. Will you excuse me a minute - or will you come along and meet him?"

"I'll wait," said Philip.

Ten seconds later, the woman's white-haired escort was on his feet. He came to Philip's table, and seated himself casually in Barrow's chair, as though Philip were an old friend with whom he had come to chat for a moment.

"I beg your pardon for the imposition which I am laying upon you," he said in a low, quiet voice. "I am Colonel McCloud. The lady with me is my daughter. And you, I believe, are a gentleman. If I were not sure of that, I should not have taken advantage of your friend's temporary absence. You heard my daughter cry out a few moments ago? You observed that she was - disturbed?"

Philip nodded.

"I could not help it. I was facing her. And since then I have thought that I - unconsciously - was the cause of her perturbation. I am Philip Curtis, Colonel McCloud, from Fort MacPherson, two thousand miles north of here, on the Mackenzie Kiver. So you see, if it is a case of mistaken identity - "

"No - no - it is not that," interrupted the older man. "As we were passing your table we - my daughter - heard you speak a name. Perhaps she was mistaken. It was - Peter God."

"Yes. I know Peter God. He is a friend of mine."

Barrow was returning. The other saw him over Philip's shoulder, and his voice trembled with a sudden and subdued excitement as he said quickly:

"Your friend is coming' back. No one but you must know that my daughter is interested in this man - Peter God. She trusts you. She sent me to you. It is important that she should see you to-night and talk with you alone. I will wait for you outside. I will have a taxicab ready to take you to our apartments. Will you come?"

He had risen. Philip heard Barrow's footsteps behind him.

"I will come," he said.

A few minutes later Colonel McCloud and his daughter left the cafe. The half-hour after that passed with leaden slowness to Philip. The fortunate arrival of two or three friends of Barrow gave him an opportunity to excuse himself on the plea of an important engagement, and he bade the Mica King good-night. Colonel McCloud was waiting for him outside the cafe, and as they entered a taxicab, he said:

"My daughter is quite unstrung to-night, and I sent her home. She is waiting for us. Will you have a smoke, Mr. Curtis?"

With a feeling that this night had set stirring a brew of strange and unforeseen events for him, Philip sat in a softly lighted and richly furnished room and waited. The Colonel had been gone a full quarter-hour. He had left a box half filled with cigars on a table at Philip's elbow, pressing him to smoke. They were an English brand of cigar, and on the box was stamped the name of the Montreal dealer from whom they had been purchased.

"My daughter will come presently," Colonel McCloud had said.

A curious thrill shot through Philip as he heard her footsteps and the soft swish of her skirt. Involuntarily he rose to his feet as she entered the room. For fully ten seconds they stood facing each other without speaking. She was dressed in filmy gray stuff. There was lace at her throat. She had shifted the thick bright coils of her hair to the crown of her head; a splendid glory of hair, he thought. Her cheeks were flushed, and with her hands against her breast, she seemed crushing back the strange excitement that glowed in her eyes. Once he had seen a fawn's eyes that looked like hers. In them were suspense, fear - a yearning that was almost pain. Suddenly she came to him, her hands outstretched. Involuntarily, too, he took them. They were warm and soft. They thrilled him - and they clung to him.

"I am Josephine McCloud," she said. "My father has explained to you ? You   know - a man - who calls himself - God?"

Her fingers clung more tightly to his, and the sweetness of her hair, her breath, her eyes were very close as she waited.

"Yes, I know a man who calls himself Peter God."

"Tell me - what he is like?" she whispered. "He is tall - like you?"

"No. He is of medium height."

"And his hair? It is dark - dark like yours?"

"No. It is blond, and a little gray."

"And he is young - younger than you?"

"He is older."

"And his eyes - are dark?"

He felt rather than heard the throbbing of her heart as she waited for him to reply. There was a reason why he would never forget Peter God's eyes.

"Sometimes I thought they were blue, and sometimes gray," he said; and at that she dropped his hands with a strange little cry, and stood a step back from him, a joy which she made no effort to keep from him flaming in her face.

It was a look which sent a sudden hopelessness through Curtis - a stinging pang of jealousy. This night had set wild and tumultous emotions aflame in his breast. He had come to Josephine McCloud like one in a dream. In an hour he had placed her above all other women in the world, and in that hour the little gods of fate had brought him to his knees in the worship of a woman. The fact did not seem unreal to him. Here was the woman, and he loved her. And his heart sank like a heavily weighted thing when he saw the transfiguration of joy that came into her face when he said that Peter God's eyes were not dark, but were sometimes blue and sometimes gray.

"And this Peter God?" he said, straining to make his voice even. "What is he to you?"

His question cut her like a knife. The wild color ebbed swiftly out of her cheeks. Into her eyes swept a haunting fear which he was to see and wonder at more than once. It was as if he had done something to frighten her. "We - my father and I - are interested in him," she said. Her words cost her a visible effort. He noticed a quick throbbing in her throat, just above the filmy lace. "Mr. Curtis, won't you pardon this - this betrayal of excitement in myself? It must be unaccountable to you. Perhaps a little later you will understand. We are imposing on you by not confiding in you what this interest is, and I beg you to forgive me. But there is a reason. Will you believe me? There is a reason."

Her hands rested lightly on Philip's arm. Her eyes implored him.

"I will not ask for confidences which you are not free to give," he said gently.

He was rewarded by a soft glow of thankfulness.

"I cannot make you understand how much that means to me," she cried tremblingly. "And you will tell us about Peter God? Father - "

She turned.

Colonel McCloud had reentered the room.

With the feeling of one who was not quite sure that he was awake, Philip paused under a street lamp ten minutes after leaving the McCloud apartments, and looked at his watch. It was a quarter of two o'clock. A low whistle of surprise fell from his lips. For three hours he had been with Colonel McCloud and his daughter. It had seemed like an hour. He still felt the thrill of the warm, parting pressure of Josephine's hand; he saw the gratitude in her eyes; he heard her voice, low and tremulous, asking him to come again to-morrow evening. His brain was in a strange whirl of excitement, and he laughed - laughed with gladness which he had not felt before in all the days of his life.

He had told a great many things about Peter God that night; of the man's life in the little cabin, his loneliness, his aloofness, and the mystery of him. Philip had asked no questions of Josephine and her father, and more than once he had caught that almost tender gratitude in Josephine's eyes. And at least twice he had seen the swift, haunting fear - the first time when he told of Peter God's coming and goings at Port MacPherson, and again when he mentioned a patrol of the Royal Northwest Mounted Police that had passed Peter God's cabin while Philip was there, laid up during those weeks of darkness and storm with a fractured leg.

Philip told how tenderly Peter God nursed him, and

how their acquaintance grew into brotherhood during the long gray nights when the stars gleamed like pencil-points and the foxes yapped incessantly. He had seen the dewy shimmer of tears in Josephine's eyes. He had noted the tense lines in Colonel McCloud's face. But he had asked them no questions, he had made no effort to unmask the secret which they so evidently desired to keep from him.

Now, alone in the cool night, he asked himself a hundred questions, and yet with a feeling that he understood a great deal of what they had kept from him. Something had whispered to him then - and whispered to him now - that Peter God was not Peter God's right name, and that to Josephine McCloud and her father he was a brother and a son. This thought, so long as he could think it without a doubt, filled his cup of hope to overflowing. But the doubt persisted. It was like a spark that refused to go out. Who was Peter God? What was Peter God, the half-wild fox-hunter, to Josephine McCloud? Yes - he could be but that one thing! A brother. A black sheep. A wanderer. A son who had disappeared - and was now found. But if he was that, only that, why would they not tell him? The doubt sputtered up again.

Philip did not go to bed. He was anxious for the day, and the evening that was to follow. A woman had unsettled his world. His mica mountain became an unimportant reality. Barrow's greatness no longer loomed up for him. He walked until he was tired, and it was dawn when he went to his hotel. He was like a boy living in the anticipation of a great promise - restless, excited, even feverishly anxious all day. He made inquiries about Colonel James McCloud at his hotel. No one knew him, or had even heard of him. His name was not in the city directory or the telephone directory. Philip made up his mind that Josephine and her father were practically strangers in the city, and that they had come from Canada - probably Montreal, for he remembered the stamp on the box of cigars.

That night, when he saw Josephine again, he wanted to reach out his arms to her. He wanted to make her understand how completely his wonderful love possessed him, and how utterly lost he was without her. She was dressed in simple white - again with that bank of filmy lace at her throat. Her hair was done in those lustrous, shimmering coils, so bright and soft that he would have given a tenth of his mica mountain to touch them with his hands. And she was glad to see him. Her eagerness shone in her eyes, in the warm flush of her cheeks, in the joyous tremble of her voice.

That night, too, passed like a dream - a dream in paradise for Philip. For a long time they sat alone, and Josephine herself brought him the box of cigars, and urged him to smoke. They talked again about the North, about Fort MacPherson - where it was, what it was, and how one got to it through a thousand miles or so of wilderness. He told her of his own adventures, how for many years he had sought for mineral treasure and at last had found a mica mountain.

"It's close to Fort MacPherson," he explained.

"We can work it from the Mackenzie. I expect to start back some time in August."

She leaned toward him, last night's strange excitement glowing for the first time in her eyes.

"You are going back? You will see Peter God?"

In her eagerness she laid a hand on his arm.

"I am going back. It would be possible to see Peter God."

The touch of her hand did not lighten the weight that was tugging again at his heart.

"Peter God's cabin is a hundred miles from Fort MacPherson," he added. "He will be hunting foxes by the time I get there."

"You mean - it will be winter."

"Yes. It is a long journey. And" - he was looking at her closely as he spoke - "Peter God may not be there when I return. It is possible he may have gone into another part of the wilderness."

He saw her quiver as she drew back.

"He has been there - for seven - years," she said, as if speaking to herself. "He would not move - now!"

"No; I don't think he would move now."

His own voice was low, scarcely above a whisper, and she looked at him quickly and strangely, a flush in her cheeks.

It was late when he bade her good-night. Again he felt the warm thrill of her hand as it lay in his. The next afternoon he was to take her driving.

The days and weeks that followed these first meetings with Josephine McCloud were weighted with many things for Philip. Neither she nor her father enlightened him about Peter God. Several times he believed that Josephine was on the point of confiding in him, but each time there came that strange fear in her eyes, and she caught herself.

Philip did not urge. He asked no questions that might be embarrassing. He knew, after the third week had passed, that Josephine could no longer be unconscious of his love, even though the mystery of Peter God restrained him from making a declaration of it. There was not a day in the week that they did not see each other. They rode together. The three frequently dined together. And still more frequently they passed the evenings in the McCloud apartments. Philip had been correct in his guess - they were from Montreal. Beyond that fact he learned little.

As their acquaintance became closer and as Josephine saw in Philip more and more of that something which he had not spoken, a change developed in her. At first it puzzled and then alarmed him. At times she seemed almost frightened. One evening, when his love all but trembled on his lips, she turned suddenly white.

It was the middle of July before the words came from him at last. In two or three weeks he was starting for the North. It was evening, and they were alone in the big room, with the cool breeze from the lake drifting in upon them. He made no effort to touch her as he told her of his love, but when he had done, she knew that a strong man had laid his heart and his soul at her feet.

He had never seen her whiter. Her hands were clasped

James Oliver Curwood

tightly in her lap. There was a silence in which he did not breathe. Her answer came so low that he leaned forward to hear.

"I am sorry," she said. "It is my fault - that you love me. I knew. And yet I let you come again and again. I have done wrong. It is not fair - now - for me to tell you to go - without a chance. You - would want me if I did not love you? You would marry me if I did not love you?"

His heart pounded. He forgot everything but that he loved this woman with a love beyond his power to reason.

"I don't think that I could live without you now, Josephine," he cried in a low voice. "And I swear to make you love me. It must come. It is inconceivable that I cannot make you love me - loving you as I do."

She looked at him clearly now. She seemed suddenly to become tense and vibrant with a new and wonderful strength.

"I must be fair with you," she said. "You are a man whose love most women would be proud to possess. And yet - it is not in my power to accept that love, or give myself to you. There is another to whom you must go."

"And that is - "

"Peter God!"

It was she who leaned forward now, her eyes burning, her bosom rising and falling with the quickness of her breath.

"You must go to Peter God," she said. "You must take a letter to him - from me. And it will be for him - for Peter God - to say whether I am to be your wife. You are honorable. You will be fair with me. You will take the letter to him. And I will be fair with you. I will be your wife, I will try hard to care for you - if Peter God - says - "

Her voice broke. She covered her face, and for a moment, too stunned to speak, Philip looked at her while her slender form trembled with sobs. She had bowed her head, and for the first time he reached out and laid his hand upon the soft glory of her hair. Its touch set aflame every fiber in him. Hope swept through him, crushing his fears like a juggernaut. It would be a simple task to go to Peter God! He was tempted to take her in his arms. A moment more, and he would have caught her to him, but the weight of his hand on her head roused her, and she raised her face, and drew back. His arms were reaching out. She saw what was in his eyes.

"Not now," she said. "Not until you have gone to him. Nothing in the world will be too great a reward for you if you are fair with me, for you are taking a chance. In the end you may receive nothing. For if Peter God says that I cannot be your wife, I cannot. He must be the arbiter. On those conditions, will you go?"

"Yes, I will go," said Philip.

It was early in August when Philip reached Edmonton. From there he took the new line of rail to Athabasca Landing; it was September when he arrived at Fort

McMurray and found Pierre Gravois, a half-breed, who was to accompany him by canoe up to Fort MacPherson. Before leaving this final outpost, whence the real journey into the North began, Philip sent a long letter to Josephine.

Two days after he and Pierre had started down the Mackenzie, a letter came to Fort McMurray for Philip. "Long" La Brie, a special messenger, brought it from Athabasca Landing. He was too late, and he had no instructions - and had not been paid - to go farther.

Day after day Philip continued steadily northward. He carried Josephine's letter to Peter God in his breast pocket, securely tied in a little waterproof bag. It was a thick letter, and time and again he held it in his hand, and wondered why it was that Josephine could have so much to say to the lonely fox-hunter up on the edge of the Barren.

One night, as he sat alone by their fire in the chill of September darkness, he took the letter from its sack and saw that the contents of the bulging envelope had sprung one end of the flap loose. Before he went to bed Pierre had set a pail of water on the coals. A cloud of steam was rising from it. Those two things - the steam and the loosened flap - sent a thrill through Philip. What was in the letter? What had Josephine McCloud written to Peter God?

He looked toward sleeping Pierre; the pail of water began to bubble and sing - he drew a tense breath, and rose to his feet. In thirty seconds the steam rising from the pail would free the rest of the flap. He could read the letter, and reseal it.

And then, like a shock, came the thought of the few notes Josephine had written to him. On each of them she had never failed to stamp her seal in a lavender-colored wax. He had observed that Colonel McCloud always used a seal, in bright red. On this letter to Peter God there was no seal! She trusted him. Her faith was implicit. And this was her proof of it. Under his breath he laughed, and his heart grew warm with new happiness and hope. "I have faith in you," she had said, at parting; and now, again, out of the letter her voice seemed to whisper to him, "I have faith in you."

He replaced the letter in its sack, and crawled between his blankets close to Pierre.

That night had seen the beginning of his struggle with himself. This year, autumn and winter came early in the North country. It was to be a winter of terrible cold, of deep snow, of famine and pestilence - the winter of 1910. The first oppressive gloom of it added to the fear and suspense that began to grow in Philip.

For days there was no sign of the sun. The clouds hung low. Bitter winds came out of the North, and nights these winds wailed desolately through the tops of the spruce under which they slept. And day after day and night after night the temptation came upon him more strongly to open the letter he was carrying to Peter God.

He was convinced now that the letter - and the letter alone - held his fate, and that he was acting blindly. Was this justice to himself? He wanted Josephine. He wanted her above all else in the world. Then why should he not fight for her - in his own way? And to do that he must read the letter. To know its contents would mean - Josephine. If there was nothing in it that would stand between them, he would have done no wrong, for he would still take it on to Peter God. So he argued. But if the letter jeopardized his chances of possessing her, his knowledge of what it contained would give him an opportunity to win in another way. He could even answer it himself and take back to her false word from Peter God, for seven frost-biting years along the edge of the Barren had surely changed Peter God's handwriting. His treachery, if it could be called that, would never be discovered. And it would give him Josephine.

This was the temptation. The power that resisted it was the spirit of that big, clean, fighting North which makes men out of a beginning of flesh and bone. Ten years of that North had seeped into Philip's being. He hung on. It was November when he reached Port MacPherson, and he had not opened the letter.

Deep snows fell, and fierce blizzards shot like gunblasts from out of the Arctic. Snow and wind were not what brought the deeper gloom and fear to Fort MacPherson. La mort rouge, smallpox, - the "red death," - was galloping through the wilderness. Rumors were first verified by facts from the Dog Eib Indians. A quarter of them were down with the scourge of the Northland. From Hudson's Bay on the east to the Great Bear on the west, the fur posts were sending out their runners, and a hundred Paul Reveres of the forests were riding swiftly behind their dogs to spread the warning. On the afternoon of the day Philip left for the cabin of Peter God, a patrol of the Royal Mounted came in on snowshoes from the South, and voluntarily went into quarantine.

Philip traveled slowly. For three days and nights the air was filled with the "Arctic dust" snow that was hard as flint and stung like shot; and it was so cold that he paused frequently and built small fires, over which he filled his lungs with hot air and smoke. He knew what it meant to have the lungs "touched" - sloughing away in the spring, blood-spitting, and certain death.

On the fourth day the temperature began to rise; the fifth it was clear, and thirty degrees warmer. His thermometer had gone to sixty below zero. It was now thirty below.

It was the morning of the sixth day when he reached the thick fringe of stunted spruce that sheltered Peter God's cabin. He was half blinded. The snow-filled blizzards cut his face until it was swollen and purple. Twenty paces from Peter God's cabin he stopped, and stared, and rubbed his eyes - and rubbed them again - as though not quite sure his vision was not playing him a trick.

A cry broke from his lips then. Over Peter God's door there was nailed a slender sapling, and at the end of that sapling there floated a tattered, windbeaten red rag. It was the signal. It was the one voice common to all the wilderness - a warning to man, woman and child, white or red, that had come down through the centuries. Peter God was down with the smallpox!

For a few moments the discovery stunned him. Then he was filled with a chill, creeping horror. Peter God was sick with the scourge. Perhaps he was dying. It might be - that he was dead. In spite of the terror of the thing ahead of him, he thought of Josephine. If Peter God was dead -

Above the low moaning of the wind in the spruce tops he cursed himself. He had thought a crime, and he clenched his mittened hands as he stared at the one window of the cabin. His eyes shifted upward. In the air was a filmy, floating gray. It was smoke coming from the chimney. Peter God was not dead.

Something kept him from shouting Peter God's name, that the trapper might come to the door. He went to the window, and looked in. For a few moments he could see nothing. And then, dimly, he made out the cot against the wall. And Peter God sat on the cot, hunched forward, his head in his hands. With a quick breath Philip turned to the door, opened it, and entered the cabin. Peter God staggered to his feet as the door opened. His eyes were wild and filled with fever.

"You - Curtis!" he cried huskily. "My God, didn't you see the flag?"

"Yes."

Philip's half-frozen features were smiling, and now he was holding out a hand from which he had drawn his mitten.

"Lucky I happened along just now, old man. You've got it, eh?"

Peter God shrank back from the other's outstretched hand.

"There's time," he cried, pointing to the door.

"Don't breathe this air. Get out. I'm not bad yet - but it's smallpox, Curtis!"

"I know it," said Philip, beginning to throw off his hood and coat. "I'm not afraid of it. I had a touch of it three years ago over on the Gray Buzzard, so I guess I'm immune. Besides, I've come two thousand miles to see you, Peter God - two thousand miles to bring you a letter from Josephine McCloud."

For ten seconds Peter God stood tense and motionless. Then he swayed forward.

"A letter - for Peter God - from Josephine McCloud?" he gasped, and held out his hands.

An hour later they sat facing each other - Peter God and Curtis. The beginning of the scourge betrayed itself in the red flush of Peter God's face, and the fever in his eyes. But he was calm. For many minutes he had spoken in a quiet, even voice, and Philip Curtis sat with scarcely a breath and a heart that at times had risen in his throat to choke him. In his hand Peter God held the pages of the letter he had read.

Now he went on:

"So I'm going to tell it all to you, Curtis - because I know that you are a man. Josephine has left nothing out. She has told me of your love, and of the reward she has promised you - if Peter God sends back a certain word. She says frankly that she does not love you, but that she honors you above all men - except her father, and one other. That other, Curtis, is myself. Years ago the woman you love - was my wife."

Peter God put a hand to his head, as if to cool the fire that was beginning to burn him up.

"Her name wasn't Mrs. Peter God," he went on, and a smile fought grimly on his lips. "That's the one thing I won't tell you, Curtis - my name. The story itself will be enough.

"Perhaps there were two other people in the world happier than we. I doubt it. I got into politics. I made an enemy, a deadly enemy. He was a blackmailer, a thief, the head of a political ring that lived on graft. Through my efforts he was exposed, And then he laid for me - and he got me.

"I must give him credit for doing it cleverly and completely. He set a trap for me, and a woman helped him. I won't go into details. The trap sprung, and it caught me. Even Josephine could not be made to believe in my innocence; so cleverly was the trap set that my best friends among the newspapers could find no excuse for me.

"I have never blamed Josephine for what she did after that. To all the world, and most of all to her, I was caught red-handed. I knew that she loved me even as she was divorcing me. On the day the divorce was given to her, my brain went bad. The world turned red, and then black, and then red again. And I - "

Peter God paused again, with a hand to his head.

"You came up here," said Philip, in a low voice.

"Not - until I had seen the man who ruined me," replied Peter God quietly. "We were alone in his office. I gave him a fair chance to redeem himself - to confess what he had done. He laughed at me, exulted over my fall, taunted me. And so - I killed him."

He rose from his chair and stood swaying. He was not excited.

"In his office, with his dead body at my feet, I wrote a note to Josephine," he finished. "I told her what I had done, and again I swore my innocence. I wrote her that some day she might hear from me, but not under my right name, as the law would always be watching for me. It was ironic that on that human cobra's desk there lay an open Bible, open at the Book of Peter, and involuntarily I wrote the words to Josephine - PETER GOD. She has kept my secret, while the law has hunted for me. And this - "

He held the pages of the letter out to Philip.

"Take the letter - go outside - and read what she has written," he said. "Come back in half an hour. I want to think."

Back of the cabin, where Peter God had piled his winter's fuel, Philip read the letter; and at times the soul within him seemed smothered, and at times it quivered with a strange and joyous emotion.

At last vindication had come for Peter God, and before he had read a page of the letter Philip understood why it was that Josephine had sent him with it into the North. For nearly seven years she had known of Peter God's innocence of the thing for which she had divorced him. The woman - the dead man's accomplice - had told her the whole story, as Peter God a few minutes before had told it to Curtis; and during those seven years she had traveled the world seeking for him - the man who bore the name of Peter God.

Each night she had prayed God that the next day she might find him, and now that her prayer had been answered, she begged that she might come to him, and share with him for all time a life away from the world they knew.

The woman breathed like life in the pages Philip read; yet with that wonderful message to Peter God she pilloried herself for those red and insane hours in which she had lost faith in him. She had no excuse for herself, except her great love; she crucified herself, even as she held out her arms to him across that thousand miles of desolation. Frankly she had written of the great price she was offering for this one chance of life and happiness. She told of Philip's love, and of the reward she had offered him should Peter God find that in his heart love had died for her. Which should it be?

Twice Philip read that wonderful message he had brought into the North, and he envied Peter God the outlaw.

The thirty minutes were gone when he entered the cabin. Peter God was waiting for him. He motioned him to a seat close to him.

"You have read it?" he asked.

Philip nodded. In these moments he did not trust himself to speak. Peter God understood. The flush was deeper in his face; his eyes burned brighter with the fever; but of the two he was the calmer, and his voice was steady.

" I haven't much time, Curtis," he said, and he smiled

faintly as he folded the pages of the letter, "My head is cracking. But I've thought it all out, and you've got to go back to her - and tell her that Peter God is dead."

A gasp broke from Philip's lips. It was his only answer.

"It's - best," continued Peter God, and he spoke more slowly, but firmly. "I love her, Curtis. God knows that it's been only my dreams of her that have kept me alive all these years. She wants to come to me, but it's impossible. I'm an outlaw. The law won't excuse my killing of the cobra. We'd have to hide. All our lives we'd have to hide. And - some day - they might get me. There's just one thing to do. Go back to her. Tell her Peter God is dead. And - make her happy - if you can."

For the first time something rose and overwhelmed the love in Philip's breast.

"She wants to come to you," he cried, and he leaned toward Peter God, white-faced, clenching his hands. "She wants to come!" he repeated. "And the law won't find you. It's been seven years - and God knows no word will ever go from me. It won't find you. And if it should, you can fight it together, you and Josephine."

Peter God held out his hands.

"Now I know I need have no fear in sending you back," he said huskily. "You're a man. And you've got to go. She can't come to me, Curtis. It would kill her - this life. Think of a winter here - madness - the yapping of the foxes - "

He put a hand to his head, and swayed.

"You've got to go. Tell her Peter God is dead - "

Philip sprang forward as Peter God crumpled down on his bunk.

After that came the long dark hours of fever and delirium. They crawled along into days, and day and night Philip fought to keep life in the body of the man who had given the world to him, for as the fight continued he began more and more to accept Josephine as his own. He had come fairly. He had kept his pledge. And Peter God had spoken.

"You must go. You must tell her Peter God is dead."

And Philip began to accept this, not altogether as his joy, but as his duty. He could not argue with Peter God when he rose from his sick bed. He would go back to Josephine.

For many days he and Peter God fought with the "red death" in the little cabin. It was a fight which he could never forget. One afternoon - to strengthen himself for the terrible night that was coming - he walked several miles back into the stunted spruce on his snowshoes. It was mid-afternoon when he returned with a haunch of caribou meat on his shoulder. Three hundred yards from the cabin something stopped him like a shot. He listened. From ahead of him came the whining and snarling of dogs, the crack of a whip, a shout which he could not understand. He dropped his burden of meat and sped on. At the southward edge of a level open he stopped again. Straight ahead of him was the cabin. A hundred yards to the right of him was a dog team and a driver. Between the team and the cabin a hooded and coated figure was running in the direction of the danger signal on the sapling pole.

With a cry of warning Philip darted in pursuit. He overtook the figure at the cabin door. His hand caught it by the arm. It turned - and he stared into the white, terror-stricken face of Josephine McCloud!

"Good God!" he cried, and that was all.

She gripped him with both hands. He had never heard her voice as it was now. She answered the amazement and horror in his face.

"I sent you a letter," she cried pantingly, "and it didn't overtake you. As soon as you were gone, I knew that I must come - that I must follow - that I must speak with my own lips what I had written. I tried to catch you. But you traveled faster. Will you forgive me - you will forgive me - "

She turned to the door. He held her.

"It is the smallpox," he said, and his voice was dead.

"I know," she panted. "The man over there - told me what the little flag means. And I'm glad - glad I came in time to go in to him - as he is. And you - you - must forgive!"

She snatched herself free from his grasp. The door opened. It closed behind her. A moment later he heard through the sapling door a strange cry - a woman's cry - a man's cry - and he turned and walked heavily back into the spruce forest.

THE MOUSE

"Why, you ornery little cuss," said Falkner, pausing with a forkful of beans half way to his mouth. "Where in God A'mighty's name did YOU come from?"

It was against all of Jim's crude but honest ethics of the big wilderness to take the Lord's name in vain, and the words he uttered were filled more with the softness of a prayer than the harshness of profanity. He was big, and his hands were hard and knotted, and his face was covered with a coarse red scrub of beard. But his hair was blond, and his eyes were blue, and just now they were filled with unbounded amazement. Slowly the fork loaded with beans descended to his plate, and he said again, barely above a whisper:

"Where in God A'mighty's name DID you come from?"

There was nothing human in the one room of his wilderness cabin to speak of. At the first glance there was nothing alive in the room, with the exception of Jim Falkner himself. There was not even a dog, for Jim had lost his one dog weeks before. And yet he spoke, and his eyes glistened, and for a full minute after that he sat as motionless as a rock. Then something moved - at the farther end of the rough board table. It was a mouse - a soft, brown, bright-eyed little mouse, not as large as his thumb. It was not like the mice Jim had been accustomed to see in the North woods, the larger, sharp-nosed, rat-like creatures which sprung his traps now and then, and he gave a sort of gasp through his beard.

"I'm as crazy as a loon if it isn't a sure-enough down-home mouse, just like we used to catch in the kitchen down in Ohio," he told himself. And for the third time he asked. "Now where in God A'mighty's name DID YOU come from?"

The mouse made no answer. It had humped itself up into a little ball, and was eyeing Jim with the keenest of suspicion.

"You're a thousand miles from home, old man," Falkner addressed it, still without a movement. "You're a clean thousand miles straight north of the kind o' civilization you was born in, and I want to know how you got here. By George - is it possible - you got mixed up in that box of stuff SHE sent up? Did you come from HER?"

He made a sudden movement, as if he expected an answer, and in a flash the mouse had scurried off the table and had disappeared under his bunk.

"The little cuss!" said Falkner. "He's sure got his nerve!"

He went on eating his beans, and when he had done he lighted a lamp, for the half Arctic darkness was falling early, and began to clear away the dishes. When he had done he put a scrap of bannock and a few beans on the corner of the table.

　　　　James Oliver Curwood

"I'll bet he's hungry, the little cuss," he said. "A thousand miles - in that box!"

He sat down close to the sheet-iron box stove, which was glowing red-hot, and filled his pipe. Kerosene was a precious commodity, and he had turned down the lamp wick until he was mostly in gloom. Outside a storm was wailing down across the Barrens from the North. He could hear the swish of the spruce-boughs overhead, and those moaning, half-shrieking sounds that always came with storm from out of the North, and sometimes fooled even him into thinking they were human cries. They had seemed more and more human to him during the past three days, and he was growing afraid. Once or twice strange thoughts had come into his head, and he had tried to fight them down. He had known of men whom loneliness had driven mad - and he was terribly lonely. He shivered as a piercing blast of wind filled with a mourning wail swept over the cabin.

And that day, too, he had been taken with a touch of fever. It burned more hotly in his blood to-night, and he knew that it was the loneliness - the emptiness of the world about him, the despair and black foreboding that came to him with the first early twilights of the Long Night. For he was in the edge of that Long Night. For weeks he would only now and then catch a glimpse of the sun. He shuddered.

A hundred and fifty miles to the south and east there was a Hudson's Bay post. Eighty miles south was the nearest trapper's cabin he knew of. Two months before he had gone down to the post, with a thick beard to cover his face, and had brought back supplies - and the box. His wife had sent up the box to him, only it had come to him as "John Blake" instead of Jim Falkner, his right name. There were things in it for him to wear, and pictures of the sweet-faced wife who was still filled with prayer and hope for him, and of the kid, their boy. "He is walking now," she had written to him, "and a dozen times a day he goes to your picture and says 'Pa-pa - Pa-pa' - and every night we talk about you before we go to bed, and pray God to send you back to us soon."

"God bless 'em!" breathed Jim.

He had not lighted his pipe, and there was something in his eyes that shimmered and glistened in the dull light. And then, as he sat silent, his eyes clearing, he saw that the little mouse had climbed back to the edge of the table. It did not eat the food he had placed there for it, but humped itself up in a tiny ball again, and its tiny shining eyes looked in his direction.

"You're not hungry," said Jim, and he spoke aloud. "YOU'RE lonely, too - that's it!"

A strange thrill shot through him at the thought, and he wondered again if he was mad at the longing that filled him - the desire to reach out and snuggle the little creature in his hand, and hold it close up to his bearded face, and TALK TO IT! He laughed, and drew his stool a little more into the light. The mouse did not run. He edged nearer and nearer, until his elbows rested on the table, and a curious feeling of pleasure took the place of his loneliness when he saw that the mouse was looking at him, and yet seemed unafraid.

"Don't be scairt," he said softly, speaking directly to it. "I won't hurt you. No, siree, I'd - I'd cut off a hand before I'd do that. I ain't had any company but you for two months. I ain't seen a human face, or heard a human voice - nothing - nothing but them shrieks 'n' wails 'n' baby-cryings out there in the wind. I won't hurt you - " His voice was almost pleading in its gentleness. And for the tenth time that day he felt, with his fever, a sickening dizziness in his head. For a moment or two his vision was blurred, but he could still see the mouse - farther away, it seemed to him.

"I don't s'pose you've killed anyone - or anything," he said, and his voice seemed thick and distant to him. "Mice don't kill, do they? They live on - cheese. But I have - I've killed. I killed a man. That's why I'm here."

His dizziness almost overcame him, and he leaned heavily against the table. Still the little mouse did not move. Still he could see it through the strange gauze veil before his eyes.

"I killed - a man," he repeated, and now he was wondering why the mouse did not say something at that remarkable confession. "I killed him, old man, an' you'd have done the same if you'd been in my place. I didn't mean to. I struck too hard. But I found 'im in my cabin, an' SHE was fighting - fighting him until her face was scratched an' her clothes torn, - God bless her dear heart! - fighting him to the last breath, an' I come just in time! He didn't think I'd be back for a day - a black-hearted devil we'd fed when he came to our door hungry. I killed him. And they've hunted me ever since. They'll put a rope round my neck, an' choke me to death if they catch me - because I came in time to save her! That's law!

" But they won't find me. I've been up here a year now,

and in the spring I'm going down there - where you come from - back to the Girl and the Kid. The policemen won't be looking for me then. An' we're going to some other part of the world, an' live happy. She's waitin' for me, she an' the kid, an' they know I'm coming in the spring. Yessir, I killed a man. An' they want to kill me for it. That's the law - Canadian law - the law that wants an eye for an eye and a tooth for a tooth, an' where there ain't no extenuatin' circumstance. They call it murder. But it wasn't - was it?"

He waited for an answer. The mouse seemed going farther and farther away from him. He leaned more heavily on the table.

"It wasn't - was it?" he persisted.

His arms reached out; his head dropped forward, and the little mouse scurried to the floor. But Falkner did not know that it had gone.

"I killed him, an' I guess I'd do it again," he said, and his words were only a whisper. "An' to-night they're prayin' for me down there - she 'n the kid - an' he's sayin', 'Pa-pa - Pa-pa'; an' they sent you up - to keep me comp'ny - "

His head dropped wearily upon his arms. The red stove crackled, and turned slowly black. In the cabin it grew darker, except where the dim light burned on the table. Outside the storm wailed and screeched down across the Barren. And after a time the mouse came back. It looked at Jim Falkner. It came nearer, until it touched the unconscious man's sleeve. More daringly it ran over his arm. It smelled of his fingers.

Then the mouse returned to the corner of the table, and began eating the food that Falkner had placed there for it.

The wick of the lamp had burned low when Falkner raised his head. The stove was black and cold. Outside, the storm still raged, and it was the shivering shriek of it over the cabin that Falkner first heard. He felt terribly dizzy, and there was a sharp, knife-like pain just back of his eyes. By the gray light that came through the one window he knew that what was left of Arctic day had come. He rose to his feet, and staggered about like a drunken man as he rebuilt the fire, and he tried to laugh as the truth dawned upon him that he had been sick, and that he had rested for hours with his head on the table. His back seemed broken. His legs were numb, and hurt when he stepped on them. He swung his arms a little to bring back circulation, and rubbed his hands over the fire that began to crackle in the stove.

It was the sickness that had overcome him - he knew that. But the thought of it did not appall him as it had yesterday, and the day before. There seemed to be something in the cabin now that comforted and soothed him, something that took away a part of the loneliness that was driving him mad. Even as he searched about him, peering into the dark corners and at the bare walls, a word formed on his lips, and he half smiled. It was a woman's name - Hester. And a warmth entered into him. The pain left his head. For the first time in weeks he felt DIFFERENT. And slowly he began to realize what had wrought the change. He was not alone. A message had come to him from the one who was waiting for him miles away; something that lived, and breathed, and was as lonely as himself. It was the little mouse.

He looked about eagerly, his eyes brightening, but the mouse was gone. He could not hear it. There seemed nothing unusual to him in the words he spoke aloud to himself.

"I'm going to call it after the Kid," he chuckled, "I'm goin' to call it Little Jim. I wonder if it's a girl mouse - or a boy mouse?"

He placed a pan of snow-water on the stove and began making his simple preparations for breakfast. For the first time in many days he felt actually hungry. And then all at once he stopped, and a low cry that was half joy and half wonder broke from his lips. With tensely gripped hands and eyes that shone with a strange light he stared straight at the blank surface of the log wall - through it - and a thousand miles away. He remembered THAT day - years ago - the scenes of which came to him now as though they had been but yesterday. It was afternoon, in the glorious summer, and he had gone to Hester's home. Only the day before Hester had promised to be his wife, and he remembered how fidgety and uneasy and yet wondrously happy he was as he sat out on the big white veranda, waiting for her to put on her pink muslin dress, which went go well with the gold of her hair and the blue of her eyes. And as he sat there, Hester's maltese pet came up the steps, bringing in its jaws a tiny, quivering brown mouse. It was playing with the almost lifeless little creature when Hester came through the door.

He heard again the low cry that came from her lips then. In an instant she had snatched the tiny, limp thing from between the cat's paws, and had faced him. He was laughing at her, but the glow in her blue eyes sobered him. "I didn't think you - would take pleasure in that, Jim," she said. "It's only a mouse, but it's alive, and I can feel its poor little heart beating!"

They had saved it, and he, a little ashamed at the smallness of the act, had gone with Hester to the barn and made a nest for it in the hay. But the wonderful words that he remembered were these: "Perhaps some day a little mouse will help you, Jim!" Hester had spoken laughingly. And her words had come true!

All the time that Falkner was preparing and eating his breakfast he watched for the mouse, but it did not appear. Then he went to the door. It swung outward, and it took all his weight to force it open. On one side of the cabin the snow was drifted almost to the roof. Ahead of him he could barely make out the dark shadow of the scrub spruce forest beyond the little clearing he had made. He could hear the spruce-tops wailing and twisting in the storm, and the snow and wind stung his face, and half blinded him.

It was dark - dark with that gray and maddening gloom that yesterday would have driven him still nearer to the merge of madness. But this morning he laughed as he listened to the wailings in the air and stared out into the ghostly chaos. It was not the thought of his loneliness that come to him now, but the thought that he was safe. The Law could not reach him now, even if it knew where he was. And before it began its hunt for him again in the spring he would be hiking southward, to the Girl and the Baby, and it would still be hunting for him when they three would be making a new home for themselves in some other part of the world. For the first time in months he was almost happy. He closed and bolted the door, and began to WHISTLE. He was amazed at the change in himself, and wonderingly he stared at his reflection in the cracked bit of mirror against the wall. He grinned, and addressed himself aloud.

"You need a shave," he told himself. "You'd scare fits out of anything alive! Now that we've got company we've got to spruce up, an' look civilized."

It took him an hour to get rid of his heavy beard. His face looked almost boyish again. He was inspecting himself in the mirror when he heard a sound that turned him slowly toward the table. The little mouse was nosing about his tin plate. For a few moments Falkner watched it, fearing to move. Then he cautiously began to approach the table. "Hello there, old chap," he said, trying to make his voice soft and ingratiating. "Pretty late for breakfast, ain't you?"

At his approach the mouse humped itself into a motionless ball and watched him. To Falkner's delight it did not run away when he reached the table and sat down. He laughed softly.

"You ain't afraid, are you?" he asked. "We're goin' to be chums, ain't we? Yessir, we're goin' to be chums!"

For a full minute the mouse and the man looked steadily at each other. Then the mouse moved deliberately to a crumb of bannock and began nibbling at its breakfast.

For ten days there was only an occasional lull in the storm that came from out of the North. Before those ten days were half over, Jim and the mouse understood each other. The little mouse itself solved the problem of their nearer acquaintance by running up Falkner's leg one morning while he was at breakfast, and coolly investigating him from the strings of his moccasin to the collar of his blue shirt. After that it showed no fear of him, and a few days later would nestle in the hollow of his big hand and nibble fearlessly at the bannock which Falkner would offer it. Then Jim took to carrying it about with him in his coat pocket. That seemed to suit the mouse immensely, and when Jim went to bed nights, or it grew too warm for him in the cabin, he would hang the coat over his bunk, with the mouse still in it, so that it was not long before the little creature made up its mind to take full possession of the pocket. It intimated as much to Falkner on the tenth and last day of the storm, when it began very business-like operations of building a nest of paper and rabbits' fur in the coat pocket. Jim's heart gave a big and sudden jump of delight when he saw the work going on.

"Bless my soul, I wonder if it's a girl mouse an' we're goin' to have BABIES!" he gasped.

After that he did not wear the coat, through fear of disturbing the nest. The two became more and more friendly, until finally the mouse would sit on Jim's shoulder at meal time, and nibble at bannock. What little trouble the mouse caused only added to Falkner's love for it.

"He's a human little cuss," he told himself one day, as he watched the mouse busy at work caching away scraps of food, which it carried through a crack in the sapling floor. "He's that human I've got to put all my grab in the tin cans or we'll go short before spring!" His chief trouble was to keep his snowshoes out of his tiny companion's reach. The mouse had developed an unholy passion for babiche, the caribou skin thongs used in the webs of his shoes, and one of the webs was half eaten away before Falkner discovered what was going on. At last he was compelled to suspend the shoes from a nail driven in one of the roof-beams.

In the evening, when the stove glowed hot, and a cotton wick sputtered in a pan of caribou grease on the table, Falkner's chief diversion was to tell the mouse all about his plans, and hopes, and what had happened in the past. He took an almost boyish pleasure in these one-sided entertainments - and yet, after all, they were not entirely one-sided, for the mouse would keep its bright, serious-looking little eyes on Falkner's face; it seemed to understand, if it could not talk.

Falkner loved to tell the little fellow of the wonderful days of four or five years ago away down in the sunny Ohio valley where he had courted the Girl and where they lived before they moved to the farm in Canada. He tried to impress upon Little Jim's mind what it meant for a great big, unhandsome fellow like himself to be loved by a tender slip of a girl whose hair was like gold and whose eyes were as blue as the wood-violets. One evening he fumbled for a minute under his bunk and came back to the table with a worn and finger-marked manila envelope, from which he drew tenderly and with almost trembling care a long, shining tress of golden hair.

"That HERS," he said proudly, placing it on the table close to the mouse. "An' she's got so much of it you can't see her to the hips when she takes it down; an' out in the sun it shines like - like - glory!"

The stove door crashed open, and a number of coals fell out upon the floor. For a few minutes Falkner was busy, and when he returned to the table he gave a gasp of astonishment. The curl and the mouse were gone! Little Jim had almost reached its nest with its lovely burden when Falkner captured it.

"You little cuss!" he breathed revently. "Now I know you come from her! I know it!"

In the weeks that followed the storm Falkner again followed his trap-lines, and scattered poison-baits for the white foxes on the Barren. Early in January the second great storm of that year came from out of the North. It gave no warning, and Falkner was caught ten miles from camp. He was making a struggle for life before he reached the shack. He was exhausted, and half blinded. He could hardly stand on his feet when he staggered up against his own door. He could see nothing when he entered. He stumbled over a stool, and fell to the floor. Before he could rise a strange weight was upon him. He made no resistance, for the storm had driven the last ounce of strength from his body.

"It's been a long chase, but I've got you now, Falkner," he heard a triumphant voice say. And then came the dreaded formula, feared to the uttermost limits of the great Northern wilderness: "I warn you! You are my prisoner, in the name of His Majesty, the King!"

Corporal Carr, of the Royal Mounted of the Northwest, was a man without human sympathies. He was thin faced, with a square, bony jaw, and lips that formed a straight line. His eyes were greenish, like a cat's, and were constantly shifting. He was a beast of prey, as much as the wolf, the lynx, or the fox - and his prey was men. Only such a man as Carr, alone would have braved the treacherous snows and the intense cold of the Arctic winter to run him down. Falkner knew that, as an hour later he looked over the roaring stove at his captor. About Carr there was something of the unpleasant quickness, the sinuous movement, of the little white ermine - the outlaw of the wilderness. His eyes were as merciless. At times Falkner caught the same red glint in them. And above his despair, the utter hopelessness of his situation, there rose in him an intense hatred and loathing of the man.

Falkner's hands were then securely tied behind him.

"I'd put the irons on you," Carr had explained a hard, emotionless voice, "only I lost them somewhere back there."

Beyond that he had not said a dozen words. He had built up the fire, thawed himself out, and helped himself to food. Now, for the first time, he loosened up a bit.

"I've had a devil of a chase," he said bitterly, a cold glitter in his eyes as he looked at Falkner. "I've been after you three months, and now that I've got you this accursed storm is going to hold me up! And I left my dogs and outfit a mile back in the scrub."

"Better go after 'em," replied Falkner. "If you don't there won't be any dogs an' outfit by morning."

Corporal Carr rose to his feet and went to the window.

In a moment he turned.

"I'll do that," he said. "Stretch yourself out on the bunk. I'll have to lace you down pretty tight to keep you from playing a trick on me."

There was something so merciless and brutal in his eyes and voice that Falkner felt like leaping upon him, even with his hands tied behind his back.

He was glad, however, that Carr had decided to go. He was, filled with an overwhelming desire to be rid of him, if only for an hour.

He went to the bunk and lay down. Corporal Carr approached, pulling a roll of babiche cord from his pocket.

"If you don't mind you might tie my hands in front instead of behind," suggested Falkner. "It's goin' to be mighty unpleasant to have 'em under me, if I've got to lay here for an hour or two."

"Not on your life I won't tie 'em in front!" snapped Carr, his little eyes glittering. And then he gave a cackling laugh, and his eyes were as green as a cat's. "An' it won't be half so unpleasant as having something 'round your NECK!" he joked.

"I wish I was free," breathed Falkner, his chest heaving. "I wish we could fight, man t' man. I'd be willing to hang then, just to have the chance to break your neck. You ain't a man of the Law. You're a devil."

Carr laughed the sort of laugh that sends a chill up one's back, and drew the caribou-skin cord tight about

Falkner's ankles.

"Can't blame me for being a little careful," he said in his revolting way. "By your hanging I become a Sergeant. That's my reward for running you down."

He lighted the lamp and filled the stove before he left the cabin. From the door he looked back at Falkner, and his face was not like a man's, but like that of some terrible death-spirit, ghostly, and thin, and exultant in the dim glow of the lamp. As he opened the door the roar of the blizzard and a gust of snow filled the cabin. Then it closed, and a groaning curse fell from Falkner's lips. He strained fiercely at the thongs that bound him, but after the first few minutes he lay still breathing hard, knowing that every effort he made only tightened the caribou-skin cord that bound him.

On his back, he listened to the storm. It was filled with the same strange cries and moaning sound that had almost driven him to madness, and now they sent through him a shivering chill that he had not felt before, even in the darkest and most hopeless hours of his loneliness and despair. A breath that was almost a sob broke from his lips as a vision of the Girl and the Kid came to shut out from his ears the moaning tumult of the wind. A few hours before he had been filled with hope - almost happiness, and now he was lost. From such a man as Carr there was no hope for mercy, or of escape. Flat on his back, he closed his eyes, and tried to think - to scheme something that might happen in his favor, to foresee an opportunity that might give him one last chance. And then, suddenly, he heard a sound. It traveled over the blanket that formed a pillow for his head. A cool, soft little nose touched his ear, and then tiny feet ran swiftly over his shoulder, and halted on his breast. He opened his eyes, and stared.

"You little cuss!" he breathed. A hundred times he had spoken those words, and each time they were of increasing wonder and adoration. "You little cuss!" he whispered again, and he chuckled aloud.

The mouse was humped on his breast in that curious little ball that it made of itself, and was eyeing him, Jim thought, in a questioning sort of way, "What's the matter with you?" it seemed to ask. "Where are your hands?"

And Jim answered:

"They've got me, old man. Now what the dickens are we going to do?"

The mouse began investigating. It examined his shoulder, the end of his chin, and ran along his arm, as far as it could go.

"Now what do you think of that!" Falkner exclaimed softly. "The little cuss is wondering where my hands are!" Gently he rolled over on his side.

"There they are," he said, "hitched tighter 'n bark to a tree!"

He wiggled his fingers, and in a moment he felt the mouse. The little creature ran across the opened palm of his hand to his wrist, and then every muscle in Falkner's body grew tense, and one of the strangest cries that ever fell from human lips came from his. The mouse had found once more the dried hide-flesh of which the snowshoe webs were made. It had found babiche. And it had begun TO GNAW!

In the minutes that followed Falkner scarcely breathed. He could feel the mouse when it worked. Above the stifled beating of his heart he could hear its tiny jaws. In those moments he knew that his last hope of life hung in the balance. Five, ten minutes passed, and not until then did he strain at the thongs that bound his wrists. Was that the bed that had snapped? Or was it the breaking of one of the babiche cords? He strained harder. The thongs were loosening; his wrists were freer; with a cry that sent the mouse scurrying to the floor he doubled himself half erect, and fought like a madman. Five minutes later and he was free.

He staggered to his feet, and looked at his wrists. They were torn and bleeding. His second thought was of Corporal Carr - and a weapon. The man-hunter had taken the precaution to empty the chambers of Falkner's revolver and rifle and throw his cartridges out in the snow. But his skinning-knife was still in its sheath and belt, and he buckled it about his waist. He had no thought of killing Carr, though he hated the man almost to the point of murder. But his lips set in a grim smile as he thought of what he WOULD do.

He knew that when Carr returned he would not enter at once into the cabin. He was the sort of man who would never take an unnecessary chance. He would go first to the little window - and look in. Falkner turned the lamp-wick lower, and placed the lamp on the table directly between the window and the bunk. Then he rolled his blankets into something like a human form, and went to the window to see the effect. The bunk was in deep shadow. From the window Corporal Carr could not see beyond the lamp. Then Falkner waited, out of range of the window, and close to the door.

It was not long before he heard something above the wailing of the storm. It was the whine of a dog, and he knew that a moment later the Corporal's ghostly face was peering in at the window. Then there came the sudden, swift opening of the door, and Carr sprang in like a cat, his hand on the butt of his revolver, still obeying that first governing law of his merciless life - caution, Falkner was so near that he could reach out and touch Carr, and in an instant he was at his enemy's throat. Not a cry fell from Carr's lips. There was death in the terrible grip of Falkner's hands, and like one whose neck had been broken Carr sank to the floor. Falkner's grip tightened, and he did not loosen it until Carr was black in the face and his jaw fell open. Then Falkner bound him hand and foot with the babiche thongs, and dragged him to the bunk.

Through the open door one of the sledge-dogs had thrust his head and shoulders. It was a Barracks team, accustomed to warmth and shelter, and Falkner had no difficulty in getting the leader and his three mates inside. To make friends with them he fed them chunks of raw caribou meat, and when Carr opened his eyes he was busy packing. He laughed joyously when he saw that the man-hunter had regained consciousness, and was staring at him with evident malice.

"Hello, Carr," he greeted affably. "Feeling better? Tables sort of turned, ain't they?"

Carr made no answer. His white lips were set like thin bands of steel.

" I'm getting ready to leave you," Falkner explained, as

he rolled up a blanket and shoved it into his rubber pack-pouch. "And you're going to stay here - until spring. Do you get onto that? You've GOT to stay. I'm going to leave you marooned, so to speak. You couldn't travel a hundred yards out there without snowshoes, and I'm goin' to take your snowshoes. And I'm goin' to take your guns, and burn your pack, your coat, mittens, cap, an' moccasins. Catch on? I'm not goin' to kill you, and I'm going to leave you enough grub to last until spring, but you won't dare risk yourself out in the cold and snow. If you do, you'll freeze off your tootsies, and make your lungs sick. Don't you feel sort of pleasant - you - you - devil!"

Six hours later Falkner stood outside the cabin. The dogs were in their traces, and the sledge was packed. The storm had blown itself out, and a warmer temperature had followed in the path of the blizzard. He wore his coat now, and gently he felt of the bulging pocket, and laughed joyously as he faced the South.

"It's goin' to be a long hike, you little cuss," he said softly. "It's goin' to be a darned long hike. But we'll make it. Yessir, we'll make it. And won't they be s'prised when we fall in on 'em, six months ahead of time?"

He examined the pocket carefully, making sure that he had buttoned down the flap.

"I wouldn't want to lose you," he chuckled. "Next to her, an' the kid, I wouldn't want to lose you!"

Then, slowly, a strange smile passed over his face, and he gazed questioningly for a moment at the pocket which he held in his hand.

"You nervy little cuss!" he grinned. "I wonder if you're a girl mouse, an' if we're goin' to have a fam'ly on the way home! An' - an' - what the dickens do you feed baby mice?"

He lowered the pocket, and with a sharp command to the waiting dogs turned his face into the South.

www.ingramcontent.com/pod-product-compliance
Lightning Source LLC
Chambersburg PA
CBHW030133180626
46812CB00002B/672